DRAGON DESTINY

KATIE & KEVIN TSANG

SIMON & SCHUSTER

First published in Great Britain in 2022 by Simon & Schuster UK Ltd

1 3 5 7 9 10 8 6 4 2

Simon & Schuster UK Ltd
1st Floor, 222 Gray's Inn Road
London WC1X 8HB

www.simonandschuster.co.uk
www.simonandschuster.com.au
www.simonandschuster.co.in

Simon & Schuster Australia, Sydney
Simon & Schuster India, New Delhi

A CIP catalogue record for this book
is available from the British Library.

PB ISBN 978-1-3985-0593-3
eBook ISBN 978-1-3985-0594-0
eAudio ISBN 978-1-3985-0595-7

Typeset in Garamond by M Rules
Printed and bound by CPI Group (UK) Ltd, Croydon, CR0 4YY

MIX
Paper from
responsible sources
FSC® C171272

DESTINY

READ ALL OF THE BOOKS IN THE
DRAGON REALMS
SERIES!

DRAGON MOUNTAIN

DRAGON LEGEND

DRAGON CITY

DRAGON RISING

DRAGON DESTINY

For Mira, our littlest baby dragon

The Sky

The sky is infinite. Wide and endless and unfathomable. The sky can be clear or cloudy, and it is impossible to truly predict. The sky is ever changing, its colours shifting from day into night and back again.

What lies beyond the sky?

One creature knows the answer. A creature who has been behind the sky and returned, who once soared between realms, who is waiting to take their place in the stars. But this creature was betrayed, their trust broken, and now they are too afraid to believe in anyone again. They are trapped in a prison of their own making, and until they are freed, all they can do is watch and wait.

*

When the sky falls, when mountains tumble through clouds, when one world comes crashing into another, that is when one story will end and another will begin.

The new world will belong to those who are loyal, brave, strong and true. But only if they can survive the night and brave the dawn, while remembering that together they are stronger than any foe they might face.

Their destiny awaits.

The Situation

Billy Chan felt as if the whole world was watching him.

In fact, it was only about twenty people. But they included some of the most powerful leaders in the world – the president of the United States, the British prime minister and the Chinese president. Not to mention the dozen or so journalists who had their pens poised, ready to write down every word that came out of Billy's mouth.

As he glanced around the room, he realized there wasn't a single person not staring at him. Staring and waiting for his response to the question that the British prime minister, Edwina Nelson, had just asked him.

'So, Billy?' the prime minister repeated, giving him an encouraging smile. She was a short woman with red hair which she always wore in a neat bun right on top of her head. Billy wondered if she'd purposely chosen that hairstyle to make herself look taller.

Billy swallowed, his mouth suddenly so dry that it felt almost impossible to speak. He took a big sip of water and gulped audibly. He'd never been so nervous in his life, and that included the time he'd faced the Dragon of Death.

He tried to ignore the raised cameras, ready to capture the moment that he, a twelve-year-old boy from California, told the entire world how to deal with what was currently being called 'The Situation'. 'The Situation' was that hundreds of dragons were falling into the Human Realm every day, and nobody knew what to do about it. Nobody but Billy and his friends, apparently, who were all sitting at a round table in Buckingham Palace, taking part in this historic meeting with the world leaders.

'Well . . .' Billy finally said, his eyes darting to the side towards his friends.

Dylan O'Donnell, Charlotte Bell, Liu Ling-Fei,

Lola Lam and Jordan Edwards looked back at him encouragingly. They were all from different places around the world, but what they had in common was their bond with their dragon.

Charlotte widened her eyes at Billy and mouthed something, but he couldn't understand what she was saying. He knew she wished the prime minister had asked her the big question instead.

The question of what they should do with the dragons.

It had been five days since Billy had woken up in Buckingham Palace, surrounded by his friends and their dragons.

Five days since the uneasy truce between humans and dragons had begun.

Five days since Billy had leaped into the In-Between, the secret place between the Human and Dragon Realms, to chase down Frank Albert and stop him from becoming all-powerful.

Billy had managed to steal back *sanguinem gladio*, also known as the Blood Sword, which Frank had been using to tear rips between the realms in his search for the Forbidden Fountain, a source of magic that gave items unimaginable power. Billy and his friends had special powers from magical pearls, which had been created this way.

But Frank himself had disappeared into the nether of the In-Between, and Billy wasn't sure whether he was dead or alive. Frank had drunk the golden elixir directly from the Forbidden Fountain, but instead of granting him the power he'd been seeking, it had turned him to metal. The last Billy had seen of him was his body sinking into the rising tides of golden elixir spilling out of the Forbidden Fountain uncontrollably.

The dragons seemed certain that no living thing, especially not a human, could survive being submerged in the golden elixir, but Billy wasn't sure. He'd seen Frank's eyes follow him as he'd sunk. And they'd been full of fire and an angry promise. A promise to seek revenge.

But right now, Billy had bigger things to worry about than the fear of Frank coming back from the In-Between.

Much bigger things.

Dragon-sized things.

Because all of those rips that Frank had torn between the realms had resulted in the entire Dragon Realm starting to collapse into the Human Realm. Dragons and mountain ranges and lakes and all kinds of things were falling into the Human Realm, and nobody could stop it. The only thing they could do was figure out how to live with it. And everyone was looking to Billy and his friends for a plan.

Billy tugged at his tie and wished he were wearing something more comfortable. But his mother had insisted he dress nicely for the meeting.

That was the other thing. His parents now knew his secret. And while he wasn't exactly in trouble (after all, they couldn't ground him for saving the world), they weren't thrilled to learn of his role as a dragon-riding superhero.

His mom and dad had even met Spark. Billy wished he'd been there when that had happened, just so he could have seen their faces. But he'd been recovering from his battle with Frank Albert when his dragon had flown to California to tell his parents that he was okay. The last thing they'd seen had been an international news channel's report that had shown their son mid-battle at the top of Big Ben ...

They'd flown to London straight after to see with their own eyes that Billy really was okay. His mom had hugged him so tightly that Billy had thought she'd never let him go. She'd sworn she wouldn't let him out of her sight after that, but he'd managed to convince her, and his dad, that, well, he wasn't just any old kid any more – the world needed him and his friends and their dragons. Oh, and as if that wasn't enough, he had powers too.

After twenty-four hours in London, Billy had said goodbye to his parents as they'd headed home to California, promising he'd check in regularly. So when he'd video-called his mom that morning, and she'd told him that he needed to wear a tie to the meeting, he'd agreed with her. But now he was regretting it.

Someone at the table cleared their throat, and as a rising panic started coursing through his body, Billy realized he'd been silent for far too long.

'The dragons are our friends,' he said, desperately searching his mind for something else to say – something more convincing.

'Friends?' scoffed one of the reporters. 'They're beasts! Beasts that need to be controlled!'

'No, they're gods!' murmured another reporter. 'We should bow down to them!'

'I've heard that dragon scales can cure cancer and all kinds of diseases! We should harvest them!' a third voice piped up.

A low rumble punctuated the voices and Billy instantly recognized it as Tank's growl. He must not have liked the comment about harvesting dragon scales.

Tank and the other dragons hadn't been allowed into the meeting. They were in the next room along – a gigantic ballroom, large enough to fit them all except Lola's dragon. Neptune had gone out to sea to find other sea dragons and convince them to stop attacking human ships.

Dragons had far superior hearing to humans (as Xing liked to say, they were far superior to humans in every way), so Billy knew their dragons would be listening to every word. Which was good because it meant they wouldn't have to repeat the events of the meeting back to the dragons, and not so good because they could hear comments like that one. And Tank did tend to have a temper.

'Dragons aren't gods or beasts,' said Billy desperately. A bead of sweat dripped down his forehead. He *really* wished he'd been better prepared for this meeting. Public speaking always made him nervous. He needed Dylan's charm or Charlotte's confidence, but at least his friends were by his side.

'Well, they *are* beasts,' said the prime minister. Her smile was more fixed now. 'I'm sure even they would agree.' She drummed her fingers on the table.

'Beasts with incredible power,' added President Yang from China. He was a tall, slim man with square glasses. 'Power that can apparently be shared with humans through some sort of bond?'

'That isn't how the heart bond works!' Charlotte burst out, clearly unable to keep quiet any longer. 'Only when a human and a dragon have hearts that match are they able to bond, making the dragon more powerful.'

'Well, I would like a bond like that,' said President Banks. The American President was the youngest of the three world leaders and had a wide smile that made Billy think of both sharks and toothpaste ads. 'Bring me a dragon to bond with.' She leaned back with the self-satisfied smirk of someone who was used to getting their own way.

'That really isn't how it works,' muttered Dylan.

'You can't exactly boss around a dragon,' added Billy.

'Well, we must show them who's in charge,' said the prime minister firmly. 'They're in our world and they must abide by our rules.'

'It isn't as simple as that,' said Billy. He felt really warm now. Really, really warm. 'The dragons do what they want.'

'I think you'll find they'll do what we want them to do,' said the prime minister with a smug smile just as the doors burst open.

A dozen people wearing combat gear surged in, dragging something behind them.

A caged dragon.

Everything in Billy revolted against the sight. Dragons weren't meant to be caged. This particular dragon wasn't very big, about the size of a bull, but it was radiating with power. And anger.

The caged dragon had vibrant yellow and orange

scales, and it was so bright it almost hurt Billy's eyes to look at it directly. It had two sets of wings – two in the front and two behind. The front set looked like bat wings and the back ones were sleek and sharp with edges that looked as if they could slice someone in half. Four horns protruded from the top of its head, almost like a crown.

Not only was the dragon caged, it was muzzled. Steel ropes looped around its snout so it couldn't open its mouth, but smoke billowed dangerously out of its nostrils.

The man at the front of the cage nodded towards the prime minister. 'Madame, we've successfully caught one for you. It was tough, but we managed it using TURBO technology.'

'I thought TURBO had been disbanded,' said Jordan.

TURBO was the organization that Jordan's scientist mother had worked for. It had been run by none other than Frank Albert, who had hired Professor Edwards for her knowledge of other realms and expertise in mythical creatures, such as dragons. But unbeknown to her, Frank Albert had been using TURBO technology for his own gains. After the children had defeated him, they'd heard that the entire company was shutting down.

Professor Edwards was now working with the British government and various global science agencies, trying to figure out where the next rips between the realms would appear. At first, she hadn't wanted Jordan to stay with Billy, his friends and their dragons – she'd wanted him to stay at home where he'd be safe – but in the same way the others had convinced their parents, Jordan convinced his mum that he had to do this because the world needed them. Just like the world needed her and her vital research and expertise. At this very moment, Professor Edwards was down the hall in a meeting of a group of top scientists.

The prime minister laughed. 'We couldn't let a company like TURBO, which has so much specialist knowledge and truly amazing technology, simply disappear. Yes, Frank Albert turned out to be someone we never should have trusted, but with TURBO's help, humans will retain their place at the top of the food chain ... even with dragons in the picture.'

President Banks gazed hungrily at the thrashing yellow and orange dragon. 'I'm very impressed, Edwina. I do hope TURBO can catch me one next.'

'You can't catch dragons and force them to bond with you!' cried Lola.

'Nonsense. That's exactly what we intend to do,' said the prime minister. Then she turned back to Billy. 'Now, how does one bond with a dragon?'

'Let it go!' Billy shouted, standing up. 'This isn't how you bond with a dragon!'

Suddenly, there was a blast of light and heat from the cage, and the next moment, the dragon was free. Spots appeared in Billy's vision, but he could see the dragon was now glowing a molten white. He'd never seen a dragon with the ability to turn its whole body into a ball of white-hot flame. Waves of heat rolled off the dragon as it opened its mouth and roared in anger.

'This is bad!' said Dylan. He and the others had quickly left their seats and were now standing next to Billy. 'Very, very bad.'

'I will never bond with a human!' roared the flaming dragon. 'We have come into your world against our will, but we will make our own home here.' It threw back its head and roared again, and a column of white-hot light burst out of its mouth and blew a hole in the ceiling. Government aids and journalists screamed and ran for the doors.

'Prime Minister! Get down!' shouted a man in a military outfit, helping the British prime minister take cover behind a desk. 'You too, President Banks and President Yang!'

The American and Chinese presidents both huddled with the prime minster as the security team tried and failed to control the flaming dragon.

The flaming dragon roared again, blasting another hole in the ceiling, and the entire building shook. Billy felt his stomach clench with anxiety. He and his friends were the ones claiming that humans and dragons could live together peacefully, yet here was a dragon destroying Buckingham Palace in a rampage. He quickly thought about his friends and their various powers to figure out who might be best suited to dealing with this particular situation.

'Dylan! Can you try to use your charm on it? We need to calm it down! I think it's frightened.'

Dylan groaned. 'There's no way I'm going near that

thing. It isn't frightened, it's furious! And murderous! If my charm didn't work, I'd be barbecued O'Donnell, and nobody wants that.'

'You could try to charm it from a distance,' muttered Charlotte. 'I would if I could.'

'Do I tell you how to use your power?' said Dylan.

'Yes, frequently,' said Charlotte with a scowl.

'Guys! We have to stay focused!' said Billy, his voice tight with exasperation. 'It just blew another hole in the ceiling!'

'If that dragon keeps blasting holes in Buckingham Palace, we're going to have a very hard time convincing anyone that dragons are generally friendly,' said Ling-Fei, wincing as it blew another hole in the wall.

'Friendly? That thing is as angry as a trapped hornet,' said Charlotte, slowly edging towards the back wall. 'We need backup.'

'About time you asked!' cried a familiar voice as Xing burst through the window, sending shattered glass everywhere.

'Xing! I'm so glad you're here!' said Ling-Fei, beaming at her dragon. 'We need you!'

'Of course you do,' said Xing. 'You always need

us.' Then she moved so fast she became a silver blur shooting through the air as she zipped around the furious flaming dragon in the middle of the room.

Moments later, Billy realized what she was doing. She was using her water power to douse the flaming dragon's fire. Steam rose up from its body and it roared in frustration.

Then came a sudden loud crack and the entire back wall of the room fell away. Spark, Billy's dragon, flew in and shot out a stream of ice, leaving the flaming dragon standing frozen in place.

The Dragons Of Dawn

The British prime minister stood up from behind the desk she'd been using as a shield. 'Well, that did not go as planned.'

'How dare you bring in that beast and not be able to control it! You put our lives at risk!' shouted President Banks.

'It sounds as if this is an international incident now,' muttered Dylan.

'Excuse me,' said Jordan, directly addressing the world leaders. 'The bigger issue is that the dragon should never have been caged.'

'Why are we taking orders from children?' cried the Chinese President.

'Because these children know more about dragons than you. And they are the only humans in the world with the dragon bond that you so covet.' Tank's voice echoed around the huge room.

'That one is much bigger than the small creature that was captured,' declared President Banks. 'I want it!'

'Hands off, Madame President!' said Charlotte, running over to where Tank was and catapulting herself onto his head. 'That's my dragon!'

Out of the corner of his eye, Billy suddenly noticed that the ice keeping the flaming dragon in place was beginning to crack and melt. 'Can we please talk about international protocol another time? That dragon is about to set itself free and something tells me it's not going to be very happy.'

'See, the children are sensible,' said Spark. 'You human adults would do well to listen to them more often.'

'You are all merely babies to us anyway,' sneered Xing. 'I am thousands of years old, and I've seen things your puny brains could never comprehend.'

'My brain can barely comprehend what's happening right here in front of me,' said Dylan. 'I never thought

I'd be in Buckingham Palace with some world leaders and our dragons.'

The frozen flaming dragon was trembling now and the ice casing surrounding it was quickly falling off.

'Spark, quick, freeze it again,' said Billy desperately.

'Not so fast,' roared a new voice, and a dragon Billy had never seen before flew in through the gaping hole in the wall.

This dragon was long and slender like Xing, but its scales were the same colour and pattern as the flaming dragon, creating a series of vibrant orange and yellow diamonds. It was fast like Xing too, and shot through the air like a comet, circling around the frozen flaming dragon. It moved so fast it created a vortex of wind, one that even Spark's ice magic couldn't penetrate.

There was a series of loud cracks, and the ice around the flaming dragon shattered. Tank roared and shot a fireball towards it, but to Billy's horror, the flaming dragon unhinged its jaws and swallowed it. Then it began to laugh.

'Fire is my friend,' it said. 'And now I am even stronger.' It eyed Tank. 'Your power is magnificent.

What is such a marvellous dragon doing dirtying itself with humans? You should join me and my Dragons of Dawn. We do not need humans to be strong. We take strength from each other.'

'Do not insult my human,' growled Tank. From the top of his head, Charlotte glared down at the flaming dragon.

The flaming dragon tilted its head to the side, pondering Tank and Charlotte, and then it gazed at the other dragons and the children they were heart-bonded with. The second dragon with the same scale pattern as the flaming dragon also paused and observed them. Billy noticed that it mimicked the head tilt of the flaming dragon almost exactly.

'Why do you defend the human? Did you not see the cage these humans trapped me in? They thought they could force a bond on me! You may think you need a heart bond to give you strength, but you do not.'

A whoosh of air went over Billy's head and three more dragons, all different shapes and sizes but the same colour as the flaming dragon, soared in.

'We are the Dragons of Dawn!' they chorused. 'We don't need humans, only each other!'

'This is weird,' said Lola. 'They're like some sort of dragon cult.'

'It makes me feel strange,' added Charlotte, rubbing her eyes.

'I don't like it at all,' said Dylan nervously. 'It's creepy.'

'Yes, it is very odd dragon behaviour,' said Spark.

'We are the Dragons of Dawn! We don't need humans, only each other!'

The chant echoed in Billy's brain over and over, making him dizzy. He glanced over and saw that Buttons was staring slack-jawed at the flaming dragon, clearly the leader of the Dragons of Dawn. As the flaming dragon stared back at him, Buttons's eyes began to glaze over.

'Buttons!' Billy shouted, leaping in front of him and waving his arms around.

Buttons blinked and shook his head, coming back to himself. 'What happened?' he said, sounding confused.

'That dragon almost hypnotized you!' said Dylan.

'It is not hypnosis. I am simply reminding dragons who they are. Who they are meant to be. I am reminding them that they do not need humans,' said the flaming dragon as it lifted up into the air. 'I will leave you all alive, for now. But humans, beware. Do not dare capture any dragons against their will, or there will be consequences.'

'Who *are* you?' said Spark, gazing intently at the orange and yellow dragons.

'I am known as Flame, and we are the Dragons of Dawn. We are the future.'

There was a gust of hot air and the Dragons of Dawn rose as one, bursting out of the building and leaving Billy, his friends, their dragons and the three world leaders staring after them.

Dismissed

'Well,' said President Banks, stepping forward and dusting off her trousers as if she hadn't just been cowering behind a desk mere moments earlier. 'It appears we were wrong. None of you know how to control dragons.'

'We never said we knew how to control dragons!' said Billy, his voice rising.

'But we saw it!' said President Yang. 'On the television. That one.' He pointed at Lola. 'She controlled the giant sea dragon!'

'A heart bond doesn't mean we control our dragons,' said Ling-Fei patiently. Billy marvelled at how calm and kind she was being, even at a time like this. 'As we said, it's a unique connection between a human and a dragon that only happens when their hearts match.'

'Yes, yes, yes,' said the prime minister, waving her hands. 'But I don't have time to find a dragon with a heart that matches my own. None of us do. We're busy running countries. We need dragons now.'

'There might not be a dragon out there that has a heart that matches your heart,' said Charlotte. 'There isn't a dragon match for every human on the planet.'

'Well, we simply cannot live in a society where some people have dragons and the power that comes with them and others do not,' said the prime minister. She turned to President Banks and President Yang. 'That being said, I propose we make dragon bonding illegal. On a global scale.'

'Wait, wait, wait,' said Jordan. 'Are you saying that because you might not bond with a dragon, nobody can?'

'Also, we can't just turn off our dragon bonds,' said Billy.

'I think the prime minister makes a good point,' said President Banks. 'Any human bonded with a dragon is a threat to all of humanity.'

'You are all fools,' hissed Xing. 'Do you not see the mountains and the trees and the other creatures falling into your realm? You need dragons on your side. There are many things from our realm that will not be as kind to humans as we are.'

'That dragon, the one who called itself Flame, certainly didn't sound like it planned on being kind to humans,' said the prime minister.

'That's because you put it in a cage!' said Lola.

President Banks sighed deeply and pinched the bridge of her nose. 'I will not stand here and debate with children any longer.'

'Children who saved the whole of London! And the world!' sputtered Jordan indignantly.

'And we thank you for that,' said the prime minister. 'You'll all receive, er, medals of some kind. Knighthoods, maybe? I'll ask the Queen. But the adults need to make the decisions now. Try to stay out of trouble.'

'And keep your dragons out of trouble too,' said President Banks warningly. 'We have TURBO technology and we will not hesitate to use it.'

'Hang on—' said Billy.

'That is all. You're dismissed.' The prime minister levelled a steely gaze at them, and Billy suddenly felt as if he were being sent to detention at school.

'You need us, and you need the dragons,' he said, desperate to make them understand.

'I said, you're dismissed.' And with that, Prime Minister Nelson, President Banks and President Yang strode out of the room, followed by their staff and security.

'What now?' said Dylan.

'Now, we make a plan,' said Billy. 'A plan to show the world that humans and dragons can live and work together in harmony.' He was deeply disappointed by how much of a disaster the meeting had been, but he didn't want his friends to know that. If anything, it made him more determined. If they couldn't count on the world leaders to be on their side, they were going to have to figure out how to fix this whole mess on their own. They could do it, he was sure of it. They'd faced much harder obstacles before, he told himself. 'It can't be that hard to convince humans and dragons to get along,' Billy said out loud. 'Right?'

'I don't know about that,' said Ling-Fei, glancing up at the holes in the ceiling.

'I'm guessing we can't stay at Buckingham Palace any longer,' said Jordan.

Charlotte laughed. 'No, I think we've definitely outstayed our welcome.'

'So where are we going to go?' said Lola. 'Where's big enough for the dragons?' Her lips started to quiver. 'And can it be somewhere near water? I miss Neptune.'

Lola's dragon, Neptune, was a water dragon, more comfortable in the sea than on land. In the Battle of Big Ben, she'd risen up from the River Thames, and was able to peer directly into the top of the famous clock tower without having to fly.

Billy knew that Lola could sense Neptune, in the way that all dragon-bonded humans could sense their dragons. Billy and his dragon, Spark, even had the ability to speak directly into each other's minds down their bond. Now he heard Spark's voice in his head.

It is going to be harder than I thought to convince humans to trust dragons. We do not want to put you in danger by associating with us. We would understand if you needed to separate from us.

'Never!' Billy was so shocked and appalled by Spark's suggestion that he shouted the word out loud instead of down their bond.

'Never what?' said Lola, frowning at him. 'I was only asking to stay somewhere near water.'

'Never will we separate from our dragons. We're safer with them. We need to stay together. All of us. We need each other,' said Billy.

The others all nodded.

'There's a place not too far from here, still in London, where dragons are congregating,' said Buttons. 'I saw it from the air. It's large enough for many to roam freely. And it appears to have a body of water where Neptune could reside.'

'Then that's where we'll go,' said Billy.

Just then, a piece of the fractured ceiling fell to the ground with a thump, nearly missing him.

'And I think that's our cue to leave,' said Charlotte. 'Let's go.'

Because their dragons hadn't been at Buckingham Palace, Lola sat behind Billy on Spark and Jordan flew with Charlotte on Tank.

'So where exactly is this mystical London location?' Jordan shouted. 'Does Midnight know where it is?' Midnight was Jordan's heart-bonded dragon, and the youngest of all their dragons.

'Midnight is the one who found it!' said Tank. 'You know how curious she is. She wanted to see where the other dragons were going.'

A large, hilly, green expanse opened up below them. Even from the air, Billy could see dense woodlands and several large ponds.

And lots and lots of dragons.

'Oh!' said Jordan. 'The heath! Of course.' He laughed and shook his head. 'I never thought I'd see dragons on Hampstead Heath.' Then his grin grew even wider. 'And look! There's the Thunder Clan!'

His dragon, Midnight, and her parents, Thunder and Lightning, were perched on top of a grassy hill, waiting for them. As Billy and the others approached, Thunder's and Lightning's faces lit up with joy at seeing them. And buzzing next to Thunder's head was a tiny gold flying pig – Goldie.

The Amethyst Mountain

As Spark and the dragons flew closer to the heath, Billy took in the sight below him.

The heath itself was a wide, sprawling green space with gentle hills, mossy ponds and tangled woods. And it was crawling with dragons.

Billy wasn't sure what it had looked like before the collapse of the Dragon Realm, but dragons of all shapes and sizes had made it into their home. Some of the smaller dragons were up in trees, almost like a strange species of bird. Others splashed around in the ponds. The larger ones stretched out on the open spaces, basking in the sun.

'They all look so peaceful,' Billy marvelled. He'd never seen dragons so relaxed.

'There are no threats to them right now, except for those terrible TURBO people. But it looks as if they have learned their lesson,' said Xing, gesturing with her tail towards a pile of warped metal at the bottom of the heath that had the TURBO logo on it. 'That must have been one of their dragon-catching inventions. Fools. Nothing can hold a dragon. You all saw what happened with that caged dragon this morning.'

'This has become an unofficial gathering place for dragons,' said Buttons.

'Clearly,' said Dylan. 'But, er, I don't see any other humans. Should we be here?'

Before any of the dragons could answer, there was a loud *whoosh* overhead that sounded like a humongous piece of paper being ripped in two. A hole in the sky had appeared and a pale blue dragon was tumbling out, doing cartwheels as it tried to orient itself.

Spark dodged the falling dragon with ease and sent out a burst of lightning power to catch and steady it.

A group of dragons near one of the ponds began to

roar in welcome, and one, a pearly white dragon with a long red mane running from the top of its head to the tip of its tail, swooped over to the pale blue dragon and then called over to Spark.

'This one is in our clan,' it said. 'Thank you for catching her. She was far from home when the rips started appearing in the Dragon Realm, and we have been waiting and hoping for her arrival.'

The pale blue dragon blinked and shook her head. 'Where am I? One moment I was soaring over the Amethyst Mountain, and the next thing I knew I was spinning as if I had been caught in a windstorm. Now I am here!' She gazed around. 'What is this place?'

'There is much to tell you,' the dragon with the red mane replied. 'Come, rest first, then we can talk.' The dragon glanced at Billy and raised its furry red eyebrows. 'You are a brave group of humans to come here where the dragons reign.'

Billy stared after the two dragons as they flew over to a small group lying under a copse of trees. 'What did it mean by that?'

'I imagine most humans are avoiding the dragons,' said Tank.

'I don't blame them,' said Dylan bluntly. 'Even after seeing what happened between Lola and Neptune, you'd still be worried that you'd end up as lunch! No offence.'

'No, you are quite right,' said Xing. 'It is the way of things. It is right for humans to fear us.'

'But that can't be how dragons and humans live,' said Billy.

'It is only the start of this new world, Billy,' Spark said gently. 'Peace takes time.'

Billy scratched his head. 'Why was that blue dragon so surprised to be here? Do some dragons in the Dragon Realm still not know what's happening between the realms?'

'I imagine most don't know,' said Buttons. 'Especially those who are out on their own. The Dragon Realm is so large and vast that no dragon can possibly know everything that happens across all of it. Even when it's something as serious as this.'

'Does that mean Frank Albert has sliced a hole here?' said Jordan, glancing around.

'No, it does not,' said Xing. 'Frank sliced so many cuts between the realms in his search for the

In-Between that he considerably weakened both realms. Now there are soft spots everywhere, and eventually the whole of the Dragon Realm will fall into the Human Realm. It is just a matter of how long it takes.'

Suddenly, there was a loud groaning above them, as if the sky itself was buckling.

Billy gulped. 'If that dragon fell through a soft spot near the Amethyst Mountain, does that mean the mountain is going to come through next?'

'Right in one,' cried Charlotte. 'WATCH OUT!'

The sky ruptured and a sparkling purple mountain fell from the gaping hole. The mountain plummeted down towards the earth, pinwheeling in the air, and sent chunks of amethysts flying.

Light glinted off the mountain, and Billy shielded his eyes. Spark pulled back sharply to get out of the way, and the other dragons followed suit.

'Can we stop it?' Billy cried.

He didn't know what would happen when the mountain made contact with the ground. If it had the same impact as a comet or an asteroid, the entire planet would be destroyed. He felt his heart begin to hammer in his chest and he knew they had to do something, anything. His fear crystallized into focus as he tried to come up with a plan. The mountain was still so far away, high up in the sky where it had torn through the realms, giving them a little bit of time.

'How? It's falling quickly!' yelled Lola.

'We have to get every last dragon off the heath or the Amethyst Mountain will crush them all!' said Jordan.

'And look! There are houses over there!' Dylan pointed to a street at the edge of the heath.

'We have to get the humans out,' said Billy. He turned to Xing, the fastest flier in the group. 'Xing! You and Ling-Fei need to evacuate those houses!'

Xing shot off towards the houses as the mountain fell even closer – so close now that it was blocking the sun in the sky.

'They'll never get everyone out in time,' said Dylan. Then his eyes widened behind his glasses. 'They might even be crushed themselves!'

'They have to try!' said Lola.

'They'll be fine,' said Billy, willing it to be true. 'Xing is too fast to let anything fall on top of her.'

Dragons were lifting up into the air in droves, leaving the heath and soaring down towards the heart of the city. Billy could hear the screams of humans, still unused to seeing dragons in the sky, not to mention a giant hurtling purple mountain.

'Where's Midnight?' Jordan suddenly cried. 'I can't see her! She was over there on that hill and now she's gone!'

'I'm right here!' yelled a familiar high-pitched voice. Midnight was flapping frantically towards them, Thunder and Lightning soaring protectively behind her. Midnight's spiral horns were glowing brightly and her midnight-blue scales shone. 'But we all need to get out of here! And fast!'

She flew close to Tank, where Jordan still sat, and he effortlessly hopped astride his own dragon. The strength of their heart bond meant it was nearly impossible for him to fall off her.

'Midnight is right,' said Thunder. 'Come quickly with us, further north of the city.'

Billy suddenly had an idea. 'Wait! What if we . . . exploded the mountain?'

'How exactly are we going to do that?' said Dylan.

He gestured up at the sky. 'We're running out of time too – that thing is going to land any minute!'

'Spark, Tank, Thunder and Lightning can use their combined powers to shatter it,' said Billy.

'But won't that just mean there will be even *more* falling pieces?' said Charlotte. 'If a rock the size of a baseball hits a human on the head, they're a goner for sure!'

'If they direct enough power at the mountain, they'll be able to blast it into smithereens,' said Billy.

'It's worth a try,' said Jordan. 'Otherwise that mountain is going to crush all of North London!'

Billy glanced over at the houses lining the edge of the heath and saw Xing and Ling-Fei were indeed evacuating people out of their homes, but not anywhere near fast enough.

Billy swallowed. 'Buttons, you take Dylan, Lola, Midnight and Jordan, and fly further north of the city. If my plan doesn't work, well, some of us need to stay alive.'

'We're all staying alive!' Lola said, determined. 'And I'm not going anywhere.'

'Nice try, mate,' said Jordan. 'We're staying right here with you.'

'I'm deeply offended that you think I can't help with this plan,' said Buttons. 'You'll most certainly need healing after this.'

'We're in it together,' said Dylan.

Billy grinned at the group, filled with gratitude to have them here with him. He knew how lucky he was to have friends who always looked out for each other, even in the most dangerous situations. No matter what happened now, they were together and that's what mattered most.

'Well then, we'd better move fast,' said Charlotte. 'Tank, are you ready to fire?'

'Ready!' rumbled Tank.

'We need you all to hit the mountain with everything you've got,' said Billy. 'Spark, Lightning, Thunder, you have to time it right.'

'On my count,' said Lightning, her jewel-toned scales sparkling in the strange purple light streaming through the Amethyst Mountain.

Electricity crackled within Spark as she levelled up, and Billy focused on sending her as much strength as he could through their bond.

The falling mountain was so close now, but then,

with a mighty roar, the dragons let out a blast of energy aimed directly at the mountain. As it hit it, the mountain froze in mid-air and, for a moment, everything was silent.

Then there was a crackling sound, and the Amethyst Mountain exploded.

Dragon Uniforms

A huge cloud of sparkling purple dust erupted from what had once been the Amethyst Mountain. It coated Billy and his friends and their dragons in its shine.

Billy began to laugh – he couldn't help it.

They'd done it. They'd stopped the mountain from crashing onto the heath and crushing humans and dragons alike. And now they were all covered in shining purple dust, including the entire heath – from the trees to the hills to the ponds.

Charlotte let out a whoop. 'That was *epic!*'

'I can't believe we just exploded a mountain,' said Dylan.

'Technically, the dragons are the ones who did it,' said Lola, but she was laughing too.

Moments later, Xing and Ling-Fei, also coated in the same sparkling dust, flew over. Ling-Fei was grinning.

'Well done, you guys!'

'I do not believe you made me waste my energy evacuating those humans from their homes when the mountain didn't even crash to the earth!' exclaimed Xing. Then she whipped her tail around and admired it. 'However, I will admit I like the extra shine I now have.'

Xing, like many dragons, hoarded jewels and shiny items. It always amused Billy how much a shining jewel could make Xing, a sharp-toothed and sharp-tongued dragon, melt.

'The humans will have seen dragons working to save them,' said Buttons, nodding in the direction of the houses. 'I hope this will convince some of them that we're not terrible monsters to be feared, and that we can work and live together in peace.'

A crowd of humans stood, cheering and laughing, as they wiped sparkling dust off their faces.

Billy gazed at the remnants of the Amethyst Mountain. 'But if this is going on all over the world, what's going to happen when we aren't able to intervene?'

'This is why humans and dragons have to start working together,' said Charlotte. 'Humans need dragons.'

'But dragons do not need humans,' said a new voice.

Billy whipped his head around. It was Flame, flying in close. It must have just arrived, because it wasn't covered in amethyst dust, making its orange and yellow scales stand out even more in comparison.

Spark flapped her wings in alarm. 'Bold of you to sneak up on us like that.'

'Dangerous too,' hissed Xing as she looped round him threateningly. Tank growled in agreement, and Midnight's horns glowed in warning.

Flame seemed unbothered. 'Silence is one of my skills. One that I teach all of my Dragons of Dawn.' It eyed the group. 'So many powerful dragons working with small humans. What a waste. I saw what you did, and you did not need the human children to blast that mountain.'

'Our bonds with the children make us stronger,' said Spark. 'You know there is nothing that gives a dragon greater strength than a true bond.'

'So we have always been told,' said Flame. 'But we are in a new world now, are we not? A new world, and perhaps a new way of doing things . . .'

'What do you want?' said Billy suspiciously.

'I want what I had. A land for dragons. A land without humans. Or at least only the occasional one who slips through the gaps.' Flame licked its lips. 'Those humans always made for a good treat. But this world filled with humans and their greed? I do not care for it.'

'It was our world first,' said Charlotte hotly. 'Nobody in this world asked for dragons to start falling into it.' She patted Tank on the head. 'No offence, of course. I'd always want you to be in my world.'

'And I you,' said Tank.

Flame seemed to shrug. 'I will admit that for humans, you children are not too odious. But you saw what the human rulers tried to do to me. They caged me. Tried to take my power for their own.' Hatred seeped into its voice. 'I have heard humans claim that love is their strongest emotion, but I know differently. Humans are ruled by fear and greed. That is why your world is ruined, and why your wars are unending.'

'Actually, the greediest creature we ever met was a dragon,' mused Dylan. 'You might have heard of her? The Dragon of Death? Big purple one? Sucked up the energy from, oh, literally everything?'

Flame considered Dylan for a moment before speaking. 'I know the tales of the Dragon of Death, and I know that you defeated her and restored the world. I admire that. But I propose a new way of living, a way even the Dragon of Death was not bold enough to embrace. A way without humans.'

Billy swallowed, trying to stay calm and brave. They had to convince Flame to give up on its mission to rid the world of humans. 'You live in this world now. A world with humans. Whether you like it or not.'

Flame gave him a wicked grin, all of its teeth glinting in the light. 'We will see about that.' It glanced at the assembled dragons. 'You will always have a place with me and the Dragons of Dawn. But I will never work alongside humans. If you are with them, make no mistake, you are against me and mine.' Flame bowed its head in mock submission. 'Now, if you will excuse me, I must go to meet all the dragons here and convince them to join my cause.'

Flame then dived down to the sparkling grass of the heath and made its way towards a large dragon peering out from a hole in a hill.

'I didn't even notice that dragon there,' said Billy.

'That is one of the dragon dens,' said Thunder. 'They are all around here. It is the perfect place for dragons to make a home.'

Billy watched Flame say something to the larger dragon, who was mossy green in colour and was now nodding its head. Then, to his shock, as Flame continued to speak, the other dragon's green scales began to shift, until they were the same vibrant yellow and orange as Flame.

'How did Flame do that?' Billy burst out, pointing. 'It made that dragon change the colour of its scales!'

'I have never seen such a thing,' said Spark.

'It's like a dragon ... uniform,' said Charlotte.

'Yeah, like a football kit,' Jordan agreed. 'It shows everyone they're on the same team.'

'How strange,' said Ling-Fei.

Flame followed the dragon into its den. Billy could have sworn it looked back at them with a smug smile, but it might just have been his imagination. A new worry began to nibble at him – if Flame continued to convince other dragons to join it and the Dragons of Dawn, how would they ever ensure dragons and humans got along?

Xing snorted. 'Well, nothing would ever convince me to change my scales. Mine are, after all, the most beautiful scales of them all.'

'Oh, I don't know,' said Lightning, stretching out her beautiful wings. 'I certainly like mine.'

'How many dragons are here on the heath?' said Billy, glancing around. 'And how many have scales that match Flame?'

'It is hard to say,' said Thunder. 'More and more are arriving every day. You saw that blue one appear unexpectedly. And dragons are always hard to count.'

'But I have not seen many with the same scale pattern as Flame,' said Lightning. Then she flapped her wings. 'Come, we will show you the den we have already made.' She glanced at Lola. 'We made sure it is near a pond, so Neptune will be comfortable.'

As the group followed the Thunder Clan, Billy couldn't help but feel deflated. All the excitement and pride that he'd felt after the dragons had successfully exploded the mountain had vanished when Flame had flown over, leaving only a rising sense of uneasiness in its place. Everything was escalating so quickly that they hadn't even had time to come up with a plan to fix things. It felt as if the situation was getting worse and worse by the minute. How could they convince dragons and humans to live peacefully if Flame was so set on destroying all humans?

Billy, Spark said down their bond as they flew behind Lightning and Thunder across the heath. *Do not worry about Flame. It is only one dragon. It does not represent how all dragons feel.*

Billy glanced back at the den where Flame had disappeared with the large dragon – the dragon who had already changed scales to show its allegiance and alliance.

'If you say so,' he said quietly, but he couldn't shake the feeling that it wasn't the last time they'd see Flame or the Dragons of Dawn.

The Secret Den

The hill that the Thunder Clan had chosen for their den was one of the tallest on the heath.

'Hey!' Jordan exclaimed as they landed. 'I've been here before! The views from this hill are ace.' Then he laughed. 'Although it's not as good as the view from the back of a flying dragon.'

Billy surveyed the view. Most of the amethyst dust had blown away, but there was still a faint sparkling sheen coating everything. He noticed the dragons who had flown away at the sight of the falling mountain were starting to return to the heath. Some made their way into their own dens and others stretched out on the grass.

There was no sign of Flame talking to any of them, but Billy saw at least three dragons with the same scale colour and pattern as Flame, which made him worried. A dragon with a huge horn must have sensed him staring because it looked up sharply and glared at Billy. Billy gulped and broke eye contact first.

At the base of the hill was a large pond, and underneath the hill itself, Thunder had burrowed a tunnel to create an entrance. It was large, but Billy wasn't sure all the dragons would be able to fit in ... especially Neptune.

Lola clearly had the same thought. 'Will Neptune be able to fit in there?'

'Where is Neptune anyway?' said Jordan. 'Shouldn't she be back by now?'

Lola closed her eyes for a moment. 'I can't sense exactly where she is, but she isn't too far.'

'The last we heard was that she was heading to the River Thames,' said Xing, scanning the horizon for a sign of the large sea dragon.

'I will send Goldie to find her,' said Thunder, turning to the tiny gold flying pig.

Billy laughed. 'Goldie does have a gift for finding things.'

'Don't I know it!' said Dylan, laughing along with him.

When Dylan had been taken by the Dragon of Death and hidden in a tree, Goldie had been the one to guide Billy to where his friend was trapped. Without Goldie, Billy didn't know if they would have ever found Dylan.

He held his hand out towards the tiny gold pig. 'Thanks for everything,' he whispered. 'After you find Neptune, I want you to stay safe in the den.' Then he looked at the hill. 'Back to Lola's question: how *is* Neptune going to fit in there?'

'There is a water entrance,' explained Lightning. 'Do not worry.'

'I wish there was a different way for me to get inside,' grumbled Tank, eyeing the entrance. 'I will barely fit in there.'

'Give it a try,' said Lightning with a wink. 'We might have worked a little dragon magic on it.'

'Come in,' said Midnight, unable to contain her excitement. 'I can't wait to show you everything!'

It was immediately clear to Billy that this was no ordinary den. He watched in amazement as the entrance widened to the exact size of each dragon, and then, when they were all inside, it shut completely.

'Now that we are inside the den, the outside will be camouflaged,' said Thunder proudly. 'To any dragon, or human, passing by, this will look like an ordinary hill. They will never find the entrance.'

'We enchanted it so it only lets in who we want!' cried Midnight, hopping around with so much enthusiasm that Jordan nearly hit his head on the top of the tunnel.

'We used the same enchantment that we used on our home back in Dragon City,' said Thunder. As he walked along the tunnel corridor, his moustache dragged on the ground. He nodded at Billy. 'You remember?'

'I do.'

Billy had first met Thunder and Midnight in Dragon City – a place in an alternate future that had been ruled by the Dragon of Death, the most dangerous dragon of all time. In Dragon City, humans had only lived to serve dragons, and Billy,

Dylan, Charlotte and Ling-Fei had been dragon groomers. Thunder had been one of their clients – Billy used to clean his teeth. Luckily, Thunder and Midnight were sympathetic towards humans and, along with Lightning, had joined them in their fight against the Dragon of Death.

Now, Billy smiled at Thunder. 'Let me know if you need me to take a look at your teeth later.'

Thunder let out a loud booming laugh. 'I might just do that, Billy.'

As the group made their way further along the tunnel, their surroundings began to change. It had been dark and muddy with roots dangling down from the roof, but suddenly gemstones began to wink in the walls, lighting their way, and the tunnel started to widen out. And then they were in a huge cavern, large enough for all the dragons. It reminded Billy a little bit of the cavern under Dragon Mountain, where their adventure had begun. In the centre of the cavern was a giant underground lake, the water a brilliant turquoise. It emitted its own light and cast watery shadows on the walls.

'That is Neptune's entrance,' said Lightning with a

smile. 'It is connected to the River Thames through an underground river. It also leads directly out to the sea.'

Billy stared into the glowing water. 'But . . . doesn't that mean other things, such as dragons or people, could find their way in here?'

'Only if we want them to. The lake is enchanted in the same way as the hillside entrance to the den,' said Thunder.

Right at that moment, Lola grabbed Billy's arm. 'Something's wrong.'

Billy looked over at her. 'What do you mean? Everything's fine,' he said. 'We're all together and safe in here.'

'Not all of us,' said Lola, panic making her voice crack. 'I can feel Neptune down our bond. She's scared and in trouble!'

Billy went cold. What could possibly scare Neptune? She was one of the strongest, most powerful and fearless dragons he'd ever encountered.

The water began to bubble, and Billy instinctively stepped back. He trusted Thunder's enchantment, but after everything he'd been through with his friends this summer, he knew that even the most solid enchantments and spells could be broken.

The lake water began to churn, and then Goldie burst out of the water, squeaking in panic.

But there was no sign of Neptune.

Caught

'Goldie!' Billy rushed over to the tiny flying pig. 'Where's Neptune? Can you take us to her?'

Goldie squeaked in what Billy hoped was agreement.

Lola let out a loud cry. 'She's hurting! Something's hurting Neptune! I have to go to her!'

Xing went very still, and Billy could tell she was using her seeker magic to locate Neptune. 'She is not in the Thames,' she said. 'But I think with the pig's help I can find her. Come, quickly.'

'We will stay here to protect the den,' said Thunder. He glanced at Midnight. 'Daughter?'

'I'm going with the rest of the dragons!' Midnight declared. 'They're part of our clan now too.'

'It is true,' said Thunder. 'And a clan protects one another.'

'Then it's settled,' said Billy. 'Let's go rescue Neptune!'

Billy desperately wished he had something reassuring to say to Lola as they rode together on Spark, but he kept drawing a blank. It was terrible when your dragon was in pain. And worse than that was the fear and uncertainty about what was causing Neptune's distress.

Xing led the way, using her seeker sense to guide. Xing was a seeker dragon, which meant she could seek magic and living things. Ling-Fei had a similar ability, along with the ability to connect with nature. Billy knew she would be channelling her own power into locating Neptune.

Soon they left the skyscrapers and streets of London behind and flew over forests and villages until they reached the coast. They swept down to fly alongside the cliffs that jutted out of the sea.

'I've always wanted to see the White Cliffs of Dover!' Jordan shouted from Midnight's back.

Billy scanned the sea below, trying to spot

Neptune. She was enormous, so it would have been difficult for her to hide unless she was deep in the water.

Then there was an unmistakable roar – Neptune's unmistakable roar – and Billy saw a huge wave crest up around the side of the cliff face.

'There!' Billy cried. 'Neptune's there!'

'She's in so much pain!' Lola said with a whimper. 'We have to get to her fast!'

'Be ready,' said Spark. 'We may have to battle whatever it is that is causing Neptune distress.'

They flew around the bend, and Billy let out a loud gasp.

Neptune was in a net.

And not just any net. A glowing, crackling net. A net that vibrated with magic. A TURBO net.

And next to the giant sea dragon, a boat bobbed in the tumultuous sea. It was a small black speedboat with TURBO printed on its side.

'TURBO again!' cried Jordan. 'All of this technology should have been destroyed! They're using it to harm dragons!'

'Not on my watch!' roared Tank, soaring down

towards the water and sending a blast of fire directly at the TURBO boat.

But the boat was somehow protected, and Tank's fire bounced off it, lighting the sea on fire instead.

Neptune was thrashing now, trying to throw off the glowing net that was pinning her down, but the more she fought against it, the more the net tightened round her.

'Spark, do something!' said Billy.

'I will do my best,' Spark replied as she dived closer, sending out a blast of her own electric power at the net.

But it was no use. Spark's power rebounded just as Tank's fire had when it hit the TURBO boat.

Neptune let out another roar of pain and frustration as three TURBO workers in full body suits began to tighten a chain round her neck. Billy had never thought it would be possible to restrain a dragon of Neptune's size and strength, but the chain was clearly blocking her power.

Lola screamed again as one of the workers prodded Neptune with what looked like a giant fish hook. 'We have to save her!'

Suddenly, there was a flash of light, and Flame appeared. And it wasn't alone. There were two other dragons with it, all with matching scale colours and patterns.

The Dragons of Dawn.

'HUMANS! RELEASE THE DRAGON!' Flame shouted.

The TURBO workers ignored Flame and continued to prod Neptune, clearly trying to subdue her. But even with the net weighing down on her, and the chain tightening round her neck, Neptune continued to fight.

'We can work together!' Billy cried out to Flame.

'Never!' Flame scoffed. 'That dragon does not need a human. Humans have helped enough!'

'Please! Just set her free! Anyone!' Tears were streaming down Lola's face now. 'I can't bear this!' And without warning, she dived off Spark and into the sea.

'Lola!' Billy cried, urging Spark down towards the waves.

But then a strange thing happened. Time slowed down. Billy wasn't sure how else to describe it. Time itself suddenly felt slow and sticky, like wading through syrup. Billy tried to dive after Lola, but it felt almost impossible to move. Even his eyes were slow and heavy. When he finally managed to glance down towards the sea, he saw with confusion that Lola was slicing through the water like a fish. But how was she possibly moving so fast?

Billy forced his eyes over to Spark, immediately noticing that her wings were flapping very, very slowly.

Spaaaark, he thought down their bond. It felt as if even his thoughts were moving in slow motion. *What's happening?*

Spark's response came back so slowly that Billy wondered if he was imagining it.

Time. Time is slowing down.

Billy tried to make sense of the words. What did that even mean? Was this a TURBO trick?

In a haze, Billy saw Lola reach out and touch Neptune, and the moment she did, Neptune broke free of the chain and net.

Next to her, Flame began to blow a fireball towards the workers, but it moved out of its mouth so slowly that it looked as if it could be easily batted away.

And that was what Neptune did. She pulled back her giant claw and batted Flame's fireball directly at the TURBO boat, as if it were a tennis ball she was tossing. Billy couldn't understand how she seemed to be moving so fast when everything else was happening in slow motion.

'HUMANS ON BOARD!' Billy tried to shout, but the words were heavy in his mouth. Yes, these were humans who worked for TURBO, but he still didn't want anyone to die if they didn't have to.

Then everything started to happen very quickly, as if someone had pressed a fast-forward button.

Neptune roughly picked up the three humans on the TURBO boat, holding them in her claws, and then, with a blast, Flame's fireball hit the boat. It exploded, and all of the TURBO tech sank into the sea.

Neptune held up one of the humans and let him dangle in front of her face.

'Neptune!' Lola chastised gently. 'Put him down.'

'I should eat him,' Neptune said thoughtfully. 'It would serve him right.'

'Eat him and then join us!' cried Flame. 'We sensed

your distress and we came to your rescue. We are your brothers and your sisters, even if you think we are different to you. We are dragons, and together we are stronger. You do not need a human.'

'Yes, she does! I'm the one who removed her chain!' said Lola, glaring at Flame.

'Question, how exactly did you do that?' said Dylan, taking off his glasses and rubbing his eyes. 'And how did you even manage to get to Neptune so quickly? I thought you were riding Spark with Billy. Do you suddenly have super speed too?'

Was that what it looked like to everyone else when Billy used his speed and agility power? He'd never asked his friends what they thought when he levelled up his speed. But he knew his power wasn't anything like what Lola had just done.

Before Billy could think about it any more, Flame shot towards Neptune and knocked the man out of her claws and into the sea. 'If you won't destroy this human, then I will! They must be punished for daring to try to restrain a dragon!'

'I agree,' said Lola, and the mercilessness in her tone chilled Billy. 'They were hurting my dragon!'

'If dragons start killing humans, humans will take revenge,' said Jordan. 'That's just the way our world works.'

'Fine. I will save the human,' said Xing, and she dived down and picked up the screaming, spluttering man with her tail. She glanced back at him. 'Do be quiet – I have just saved your life. There is nothing more to scream about.'

The other two humans were still in Neptune's giant claws looking petrified. With a sigh, the sea dragon deposited them both on top of the white cliffs. Then she stared at them and bared her teeth. 'I will not be so forgiving next time.'

The humans fell to their knees. 'I will tell all about the mercy given to us by the great sea dragon!' one cried.

Xing dropped the man she had rescued next to the other two. 'And me?' she said, preening. 'What will you say about me?'

The man was shivering all over. 'I will say I was saved! All will know of your mercy.'

'And of my beauty and wisdom,' said Xing.

'Xing, is now really the time to fish for compliments?' muttered Dylan.

'All will know!' the three humans cried.

'Be gone, before we change our minds,' growled Neptune. And with a final bow, the men ran for their lives.

Flame's Threat

'You fools. Why did you spare them?' hissed Flame, glaring at the group of dragons.

'We must learn to live peacefully,' said Spark to Flame. 'It is the only way.'

'It is the way if you are a fool and a coward,' Flame snarled back. 'You call yourselves dragons, and yet you do not take revenge as is your right.'

'The TURBO technology was destroyed,' said Billy. 'The humans didn't need to be destroyed too.'

Flame glowed dangerously bright. 'I am not talking to you, human boy.'

'The humans were mine to seek vengeance on, and I chose not to,' said Neptune. 'The children are right.

Humans will only ever continue the cycle of revenge. We dragons know better.'

'So you befriend the humans that harm you?' Flame countered.

'Sparing them is not befriending them,' Neptune responded calmly. 'But to declare every human an enemy is foolish. Did you not see how my human chose to save me, at much risk to herself? That is the strength of the bond. That is the goodness that can be found in a human heart.'

'Humans are vermin.' Flame reared back and looked at Neptune, Midnight, Tank, Xing, Buttons and Spark. 'I will ask you once more. Will you join me, and your dragon brethren, in making this world one fit for dragons? Will you forsake your so-called heart bonds so you can learn the true power that comes from being a dragon? Will you allow yourself to accept that you do not need a human?'

Spark? Billy asked down their bond. *Do you ... want to join them?* He couldn't help but compare Flame to the Dragon of Death – the dragon who had tempted Spark away from him.

Spark's response was immediate, firm and gentle all at once. *No, Billy. I know that humans and dragons can live together peacefully. We are stronger as a unit and I will not be swayed, no matter what this flaming dragon says.*

The relief Billy felt was palpable. Spark was still his dragon. He'd lost her once before, and the thought of losing her again had almost been too much to bear. Billy eyed the other dragons to see if any of their scales had started to change in the telltale sign that showed they were joining Flame and the Dragons of Dawn. But they all remained their same colour.

'We do not need to be enemies,' Tank said. 'You do not need to bond with a human for us to be on the same side.'

'As long as you are not causing havoc and destruction in this realm, that is. We have seen enough of that,' added Spark.

'No,' snarled Flame. 'If you are not with me, you are against me. And you will live to regret it.'

With that, Flame and the other two Dragons of Dawn flew off in a burst of white light, leaving the group alone by the White Cliffs of Dover.

Lola quickly turned to her dragon. 'Neptune, are you all right?' she said, stroking the top of the huge dragon's head.

Neptune nodded. 'I am fine. Weakened, but fine.' But the sea dragon didn't look fine, and Billy watched with increasing worry as she swayed back and forth.

Buttons cleared his throat. 'I hope I won't cause offence if I suggest that perhaps I can help heal you?'

Neptune turned her head and gazed at Buttons before nodding. 'I would appreciate that.'

'Can we go to the shore? It's much easier for me to focus on healing if I'm not flying.'

It was strange to Billy to hear Buttons being so formal, but then he realized that Buttons had only met Neptune a few days ago. They might still be wary of each other.

Neptune nodded and swam towards the nearest shore. Once there, she lay down in the surf, her enormous body rising out of the waves.

Buttons, who was significantly smaller than Neptune, arranged himself near her head.

'You know, I have never been healed by a dragon before.' Neptune smiled.

'What did you do when you hurt yourself in the past?' asked Ling-Fei.

'I would go to the bottom of the sea and wait until my wounds healed on their own. Luckily, I was never very badly injured. But this –' Neptune's tail flicked up towards the raised and angry marks left on her neck – 'this is by far the worst I have been hurt.'

'Do you not have a clan?' said Midnight curiously. 'Or parents?'

'Ignore her,' said Xing sharply. 'She is a young dragon and has not yet learned how to hold her tongue.'

'It's a good question!' Midnight said indignantly, and Billy couldn't help but laugh. He agreed with Midnight.

Neptune chuckled, the sound strange and rough, like waves crashing on rocks. 'It is a fair question. When I hatched, I was alone in the sea. I must have had parents, but I never knew them. And I found it easier to stay on my own.'

'Well, you have us now,' said Lola softly.

'And we look out for each other,' said Billy.

'Yes,' said Neptune. 'I see that.'

'You're in our clan!' burst out Midnight. 'It's a good one.'

'It is,' said Spark.

By the time Buttons had finished healing Neptune, the sun was starting to set. Neptune slowly sank back into the sea until only her head was poking out of the waves, and the others stayed on shore.

'All this excitement has made me hungry. I'm starving,' said Dylan.

Billy's stomach growled in agreement. Goldie, who had spent most of the TURBO battle darting around anxiously, landed on Billy's shoulder and oinked as if to say it, too, were hungry.

'Same,' said Jordan. 'When even was the last time we ate?'

Billy scrunched up his face, trying to remember. 'Breakfast before the press conference, I think.'

'What do we do now?' said Lola. 'Go back to London? Try to talk to the prime minister and the presidents again?'

Billy sighed and ran a hand through his hair. 'I don't know,' he said with a grimace.

'Well, I say we eat,' said Charlotte. 'We can come up with a plan over food.'

'Yes, we'll feel better once we've filled our stomachs,' said Ling-Fei. 'Can we eat here? It's so peaceful, especially in comparison to London right now.'

'London is hectic all the time,' Jordan said with a laugh. 'Although I guess it's extra hectic now.' He shook his head. 'I can't believe the Shard is gone.'

In the Battle of Big Ben, a gigantic dragon named Gar-Gar had knocked the entire building over and then used it as a sword to swipe attacking helicopters out of the sky.

'The whole city is different now,' Jordan went on.

'The whole world is different now,' said Billy. 'But I agree, we should eat first.'

'Oh, small humans, always needing food,' said Xing with an over-dramatic sigh. 'Tank, start a fire on the beach. I will fetch fish from the sea, like some sort of pelican or other undignified bird. Then the children can eat and stop moaning about being hungry.'

'Thank you, Xing,' said Ling-Fei, throwing her arms round her dragon.

Xing rolled her eyes, but Billy knew how much she loved Ling-Fei – how much she loved all of them, despite her complaints.

'We are *always* eating fish,' said Dylan, laughing. 'Who knew dragons were so excellent at catching fish?'

Xing gave him a wicked grin. 'Dragons are excellent at catching everything, but fish are the easiest to cook over an open fire. I can fly to a nearby farm and bring back a sheep or a cow if you want to try your hand at butchery?'

'Nope! No, thank you! Fish is great,' said Billy quickly.

The rest of the dragons laughed, and the sound reverberated through the evening air like some sort of rare magic.

'That is what I thought,' said Xing smugly, and then she dived into the sea. 'Neptune, surely you can assist me in catching fish for the children?'

Moments later, there was a roaring bonfire on the beach and a huge pile of fish ready to be cooked.

It turned out Neptune was especially good at catching fish. When Dylan said as much, Neptune simply stared at him. 'Of course I am,' she said. 'I am good at everything. Especially anything in the sea.'

'I was only trying to give you a compliment,' said Dylan. 'Dragons! You're so hard to please.'

'What is the appropriate response to a statement of fact like that?' said Neptune.

'"Thank you" usually does it,' said Billy, trying to hold back a laugh.

'Well, thank you for commenting on the obvious,' said Neptune.

This time, Billy did laugh, and his friends joined in. Even Tank looked amused.

As Billy and his friends sat around the fire, eating freshly caught fish with their hands, he felt at peace for the first time in a long time.

'I wish we could stay here, just for a little while,' said Ling-Fei with a wistful sigh.

'Me too,' said Charlotte. 'Right now, it feels as if we're back in the Dragon Realm with nothing to worry about.'

'Er, we always had things to worry about in the Dragon Realm,' said Dylan, raising his eyebrows behind his glasses.

Billy knew what Charlotte meant. 'But this all feels bigger. More permanent. We can't go back.' He turned to look up at Spark, who was sitting next to him, wings tucked under her like a swan in a pond. 'Right, Spark? There isn't a Destiny Bringer who can help us fix the holes between the realms? Or return dragons to their own realm? Or go back in time?' He cracked a smile. 'You know, all the things we've done before?'

'Not this time,' said Spark, and Billy noted the hint of sadness in her voice. 'The Dragon Realm is collapsing, and it is now impossible for it to ever be what it once was.'

'And here I was thinking that if we needed to, we could send all the dragons back,' said Jordan. 'You know, through a portal or something.'

'It would only be a temporary fix,' said Spark. 'Eventually, all of the Dragon Realm will be here in the Human Realm. Or it will be gone. Some things will become stuck in the In-Between.'

Billy shivered, imagining how awful it would be to get lost in the In-Between for all eternity.

'Although,' said Buttons, looking thoughtfully up at the sky, 'there's the Hidden Realm, if one believes the old tales.'

'The Hidden Realm isn't real!' said Midnight, laughing. 'It's just a story!'

'You know, I thought that about dragons once, and here we are,' said Dylan with a wry grin.

'Many stories have kernels of truth hidden in them,' said Spark.

'What's the Hidden Realm?' said Billy. Curiosity buzzed inside him. How could there be another realm he'd never heard of?

'We do not know much. It is hidden even to dragons,' said Xing.

'We don't even know if the entrance is in the Human or Dragon Realm,' added Buttons.

'All that is known about it is that it is hidden, and only one dragon knows how to find it,' said Spark. 'Glorious Old.'

Billy frowned. The name sounded familiar for some reason.

'Isn't that the name of the dragon who was slain by that sword? The *sanguinem gladio*?' said Dylan.

'Yes,' said Tank gravely. 'Glorious Old was the first ever dragon, and the first one to be slain.'

'So then nobody knows where this Hidden Realm is,' said Charlotte. 'Because that dragon is dead.'

'Well ...' said Spark, trailing off. 'Here is where the stories differ. She was indeed slain, that is known for sure.'

'But once a dragon dies, they turn into a star,' said Xing. 'We have told you this before.'

'Yes,' said Billy, glancing up at the early evening sky where the first stars were just starting to make an appearance. 'So is she up there? In the sky as a star?'

'No, she never turned into a star,' said Spark. 'The legend says that her spirit roams and that she is waiting for something, maybe someone, to help her complete her destiny.'

'Her destiny that was taken from her when she was slain,' said Xing.

'What was her destiny?' asked Ling-Fei.

'Nobody knows,' said Tank in his deep rumble.

'No disrespect to this Glorious Old dragon, but

it doesn't seem as if anybody knows anything,' said Jordan. 'Nobody knows where the Hidden Realm is or even what Glorious Old's destiny is.'

'That's because it's just a story,' said Midnight with a yawn. 'The Hidden Realm is a story, and so is the tale of Glorious Old's wandering spirit.'

A chill skittered up Billy's spine, and he looked over his shoulder, half expecting to see a dragon spirit staring back at him.

But there was nothing except the edge of the White Cliffs of Dover and the sea beyond, stretching all the way to the horizon.

A War Between Dragons And Humans

They had almost finished eating the fish when Spark whipped up her head, her eyes blazing a bright gold.

'We must get back to London. Quickly. Something has happened or is about to happen. The vision is very strong.'

'Is everyone there okay?' Billy asked, fear making his palms sweat.

'I did not see any humans, but I did see Flame and the Dragons of Dawn and an explosion where we were earlier.'

'I do wish your gift was a little more specific,' grumbled Xing. 'It would be infinitely more useful.'

'It's better than nothing,' said Buttons.

'We should go back to the Thunder Clan den on the heath immediately,' said Tank. 'They will be able to tell us what has happened in our absence.'

'We should go through the water entrance,' said Lola. 'That way Neptune can come too.'

'I can fly, you know,' said Neptune stiffly.

'Can you?' said Dylan curiously. 'I've never seen you fly.'

'I can indeed, but I prefer to be in the water where I am more in my element,' said Neptune gruffly.

'Oh, like a penguin!' said Dylan.

Neptune bared her teeth at him. 'No, nothing like a penguin.'

'Penguins don't fly at all,' said Lola, raising an eyebrow.

'They also cannot swallow a human whole and I can.' Neptune's voice had dropped dangerously low.

'Okay, okay, you're more like a flying shark then. How's that?' said Dylan.

'Dylan,' said Billy warningly. 'Don't poke the bear.'

'I am a dragon! Not a shark nor a penguin nor a bear! A dragon! One that prefers to be in the sea.'

'Got it,' said Dylan. Then he turned to his own dragon, Buttons. 'She's a bit touchy, isn't she?'

'I heard that,' grumbled Neptune.

'Well, if you can fly, Neptune,' said Billy, 'let's go.'

When they reached the den, the gemstones in the cavern ceiling and along the stone walls still glittered, providing a rainbow of sparkling light, but the place appeared to be empty.

'Where are my parents?' said Midnight, glancing around anxiously. 'They should be here!'

'I am here,' said a voice, and Lightning emerged from the shadows, unfurling her wings. Her jewel-coloured scales caught the light emitted from the gemstones, making her sparkle brightly. 'But your father has gone out to see what is happening. There is some sort of commotion on the heath.'

'What happened?' asked Billy.

Lightning sighed deeply. 'There have been ... attacks from both sides.' She paused and took another deep breath. Billy suddenly felt anxious, as if whatever she was about to say next would change everything. 'A dragon swallowed a human. Supposedly, the human was antagonizing the dragon ... but it certainly does not help dragon—human relations.'

'A dragon *ate* someone?' said Dylan, his eyes huge behind his glasses. 'I thought you guys said dragons didn't do that any more!'

'We said *we* do not eat humans. We cannot say what all dragons do,' said Xing. 'I am sure this human must have deserved it.'

'Xing!' chastised Ling-Fei.

'Fine, fine. The dragon should not have eaten a human,' said Xing, rolling her eyes.

'It is not just the dragons who are misbehaving,' Lightning went on. 'There are whispers about a group of humans who killed a young dragon while it was sleeping.'

'A young dragon!' Billy gasped. 'How could they?'

'Humans fear what they do not understand and what they cannot control. Despite what your human leaders desire, dragons cannot be controlled,' said Neptune. She had submerged herself in the lake, but her head rose out of the water as she listened to the conversation.

'I thought because there are so many dragons in

this realm now, more heart bonds might be created,' said Billy. 'Dragons and humans would be able to understand each other that way.'

'There is so much fear on both sides that even if there are heart bonds to be found, they will be lost in the chaos,' said Spark. 'If a dragon feels drawn to a human and tries to act on it, they might end up in danger.'

'Well, no humans are going to want to get near a dragon if dragons are *eating people*,' said Dylan.

'It was only the one dragon,' said Buttons.

'That we know of,' said Dylan. 'If humans are attacking young dragons, there will definitely be more dragons attacking humans too ... not that I blame them.'

Billy sighed and sat down on the ground, burying his face in his hands. 'This isn't working, is it? Humans and dragons living together. It's a disaster.'

'It might just take some time,' said Ling-Fei, but even she sounded dispirited.

'We don't have time,' said Charlotte. 'Dragons and humans are already starting to destroy each other.'

'We had hoped the human world would be ready

for us, but that does not seem to be the case so far,' said Spark.

'The problem is, a lot of humans see dragons as, and please don't take this personally, super smart animals,' said Billy.

'We *are* super smart animals,' said Buttons, blinking. 'As are you. Humans are animals too, you know. Mammals, specifically.'

Billy laughed and shook his head. 'Good point. But most humans see dragons as something they can tame or claim, not as creatures that they can live alongside.'

'And dragons see humans as an inferior species with very little value,' said Xing dryly. 'Your point is?'

'My point is that we have to convince dragons and humans to see each other as equals,' continued Billy.

'And humans have to trust dragons too,' added Charlotte.

'And dragons need to be able to trust humans,' said Lola, putting her hand on Neptune's head. 'Humans are far from trustworthy. I know that, and I'm a human.'

'You are not like the other humans . . . none of you are,' said Neptune.

'Don't you see? Even the six of you don't trust other humans,' said Billy. 'For this new world to work, for humans and dragons to live together peacefully, there has to be trust between the two groups. But I don't know how we're going to be able to achieve that. I thought that if the rest of the world, humans and dragons alike, saw us together, they'd see that it's possible. I'd hoped everyone would realize how beneficial it is for humans and dragons to bond, but now that doesn't seem likely.' Frustration bubbled through him. He had no idea how to fix this.

There was a commotion down the end of the tunnel, and Thunder's unmistakable roar rang out. Then there was a loud boom as the entrance to the den slammed shut.

Midnight whipped her head up. 'Dad's angry,' she said, eyeing the tunnel uneasily. 'Really angry.'

Everyone tensed and, moments later, Thunder burst into the cavern, looking more dishevelled than Billy had ever seen him. His long moustache was tangled and his eyes looked wild.

'Dad!' Midnight flew to her father and nuzzled him. 'What's wrong?'

'The Dragons of Dawn were trying to get into our den,' said Thunder, breathing heavily. Each time he exhaled, small plumes of smoke came out of his nostrils. 'They want the children.'

'What?' Tank roared.

'And they want to challenge you all to a battle, to show that the dragon–dragon bond is far superior to the dragon–human bond,' Thunder went on.

'There is no such thing as a dragon–dragon bond,' said Xing dismissively.

'The very concept is preposterous!' added Buttons.

'It is not a bond like the heart bond, but simply the might of many dragons. Flame is very convincing. I have never seen a dragon with the ability to make other dragons change their scales to match its own,' said Lightning in a grave voice.

Something occurred to Billy. 'Flame's power is like Dylan's – charm and persuasion.'

'Hey! I resent that. I'm nothing like that dragon,' protested Dylan.

'But its power is similar to your power,' insisted Billy.

'I'd say Flame's persuasion skills are way better than

Dylan's,' said Charlotte with a snort. 'I've never seen Dylan mobilize an entire army.'

'I could if I tried,' muttered Dylan.

'The point is that Flame is powerful. And with every dragon it convinces to join its cause, it becomes even more so,' said Thunder. 'And it gets worse.'

'Worse?' said Jordan, looking alarmed.

'The British prime minister, the American president and the Chinese president have all been kidnapped,' said Thunder.

Billy's stomach sank. He had a terrible feeling he already knew the answer to the question he was about to ask, but he still pushed ahead with it. 'By whom?'

'By the Dragons of Dawn. They want to make an example of them.'

Billy paced up and down the den, resolutely ignoring the pounding against the outer walls. Billy had hoped that the Dragons of Dawn would tire and leave, but it seemed they had no intention of going anywhere.

'So, let me get this straight,' he said, trying to keep his voice calm. 'A group of the Dragons of Dawn have kidnapped three of the world leaders, and some others are outside our den right now demanding to battle us.'

'Correct,' said Thunder. 'I would say there are about fifteen dragons outside the den, or at least there were when I returned.'

Charlotte groaned in frustration. 'How are there so many of them? The Dragons of Dawn are popping up faster than gophers in a cornfield!'

'What does that even mean?' said Jordan quizzically.

Charlotte scowled back at him. 'It means there are a *lot* of them. Too many for us to deal with at once.'

'Like that game in old arcades – Whac-A-Mole,' said Billy.

'Can we stop talking about rodents who dig holes and focus on the actual issue at hand?' said Dylan. 'The issue that a group of dragons has kidnapped *three* world leaders? And also that these dragons want us dead? Oh, and they want to battle our dragons too?'

'We can't allow the world to erupt into a giant dragon–human war,' said Lola. 'We only just survived the Battle of Big Ben!'

'Surely not all dragons want to fight humans?' said Ling-Fei. 'Just like not all humans want to fight dragons. We have to be able to convince both sides that peace is possible.'

'It is the dragons you must convince,' said Neptune. 'They are the ones with the power.'

'Neptune, you yourself were captured by humans,' said Spark. 'It is not wise to be so dismissive of them, especially not the ones who have access to power and magic from our realm, the way TURBO does.'

'A human and dragon war would be a disaster for everyone. Nobody would win. What would be left of this world wouldn't be worth living in for either species,' said Billy.

'Yeah, whoever was left would have to find another realm to live in,' joked Dylan.

'Dylan, now isn't the time for jokes,' said Charlotte. 'We need to come up with a plan!'

Billy stared at Dylan. 'Wait, what did you say? Something about finding another realm to live in?' Billy could practically feel the idea springing to life in his brain, like a car engine being switched on. He turned to the dragons. 'There *is* another realm, isn't there?'

'What are you talking about?' said Jordan.

'The Hidden Realm! The one Buttons told us about earlier!' replied Billy.

'But, Billy, that's just a story,' said Midnight.

'And even if it was real, and we could find this mysterious new realm, what exactly would we do?' said Charlotte.

'Well, it could become a home for all dragons – a safe haven away from humans. Instead of making a new world for themselves here, they could do it in the Hidden Realm,' said Billy. 'And if some dragons wanted to stay here, they could, but the ones who didn't want to live with humans, like the Dragons of Dawn, could go to the Hidden Realm. It could become the new Dragon Realm!' His words spilled out quickly, the idea becoming more and more solid in his head. 'The Dragons of Dawn aren't evil just because they don't want to live in a realm with humans. I don't blame them, to be honest. We all saw what happened to Flame.'

'And to me,' said Neptune gravely.

'Is there really no way for humans and dragons to get along here?' said Ling-Fei.

'Look at what's happening,' said Billy, throwing

his arms out wide. 'We thought humans and dragons would be able to live together, and maybe some can, like us, but not all of them. This is the only way to stop things from escalating.'

'Tell me, even if the Hidden Realm exists and we locate it, how exactly are we going to convince all the dragons to enter it?' said Xing. 'Surely they will want to stay here, having already left the Dragon Realm?'

'Well, I guess we can't force dragons to do anything against their will,' said Billy slowly. 'But if we find the Hidden Realm, and make it an option for them, hopefully they'll want to go there.'

'It depends what the Hidden Realm is like,' said Spark. 'Perhaps it is hidden for a reason. Perhaps the realm itself does not want to be found.'

'I hate it when dragons talk in riddles,' muttered Dylan.

'Spark, have you seen any visions recently?' asked Billy. Spark was a seer dragon and could sometimes see into the future.

Spark closed her eyes for a long moment. 'I am searching the future for anything that might help us, and I can see . . . something.'

'Well, what is it?' burst out Charlotte impatiently. 'That's news we can use!'

Spark slowly shook her head as her eyes opened, her gold pupils shining brightly in the den under the hill. 'My visions are jumbled. Everything is different now one realm is crashing into another. But there is one thing I have seen.'

Everyone stared at her expectantly. Billy held his breath.

'I have seen what I believe is the spirit of Glorious Old.'

A Spirit-Summoning
Jigsaw Puzzle

Dylan spoke first.

'No offence, Spark, but what are we supposed to do with that information? Isn't Glorious Old . . . dead?'

But Billy remembered the story about Glorious Old. She had been the first dragon born, the first one slain and her spirit still lingered. She was the only creature who knew where the Hidden Realm was.

'We have to find Glorious Old,' he said. 'We find Glorious Old, we find the Hidden Realm, and then we'll have a new place for dragons who don't want to live alongside humans.'

'And how do we find a dragon ghost?' said Dylan.

'It isn't a ghost, it's her spirit,' said Ling-Fei. 'Her spirit is lingering, remember? It's been waiting for something. Maybe it's been waiting for us?'

'Hmm, sounds like a ghost to me. And, again, how do we find it?' said Lola.

'By her bones,' said Spark. 'If we find her bones and piece them together, her spirit will be summoned.'

'Like some sort of jigsaw puzzle?' said Jordan. 'A magical-bone-dragon-ghost-summoning jigsaw puzzle?'

Billy grinned at his friend. 'Nice!' he said.

'I do not know what a jigsaw puzzle is, but that description sounds fairly apt,' said Spark.

'I'd like to see a jigsaw puzzle,' added Buttons. 'Perhaps after we've found Glorious Old, you children could show me one.'

'If she's real, that is . . .' said Midnight. 'But, yes, that's how the stories say to find her.' She shook her head. 'I can't believe we're going to go looking for Glorious Old!'

'Wait, you all think this is a good idea?' sputtered Dylan. 'To find a dead dragon and ask for her help? A dead dragon who surely hates humans since she was killed by one!'

'And what about the world leaders?' said Jordan. 'Shouldn't we try to rescue them first?'

'Jordan has a good point. If we go searching for this Hidden Realm, who knows what will happen while we're gone? Or what the Dragons of Dawn will do?' said Lola.

'There are still many dragons who do not want to harm humans,' said Lightning. 'The world has not completely collapsed yet.'

'Er, your world literally has collapsed,' Dylan pointed out. 'That's why we're in this situation in the first place.'

'Since we do not have heart bonds, we can stay here,' said Lightning, looking towards Thunder. 'We will not let a war start while you are gone.'

'I do not know if that is a promise you can keep,' said Spark. 'It seems the Dragons of Dawn will stop at nothing to prove that this new world belongs to them.'

'They have not convinced all dragons to join their side,' said Thunder. 'And while they are many, they are not all. Some of us will do what we can to protect the humans.'

'And who will protect you if the humans turn on

you?' said Neptune. Her neck was still marked from the TURBO chains that had held her down. 'You do not have humans to protect you, as you say.'

'My mum will help them,' said Jordan. 'She knows everything about TURBO, and she knows a lot about dragons too. I know she isn't bonded to either of you, but she'll help as much as possible.' He looked at Lightning. 'I can tell you where she lives.'

'Yes, the dragons will need a human on their side,' said Billy. 'Now that the Dragons of Dawn have kidnapped three of the world leaders, nobody will trust them without reassurance from another human.'

'We must move quickly,' said Tank. 'The faster we find Glorious Old, the sooner she can lead us to the Hidden Realm, and then we can provide a safe haven for dragons.'

'At least until we can convince humans and dragons to get along,' said Ling-Fei. 'I refuse to give up hope that it might happen one day.'

'Always the optimist,' said Billy with a smile. Then he turned to Spark. 'Do you really think we can find Glorious Old's bones?'

'We must try,' said Spark. 'I saw her in my vision, so I believe she is real and we will be able to find her.'

'I hope so,' said Billy. He turned to Xing and Ling-Fei. 'Do you two think you can help guide us to her bones using your seeker powers?'

'It will take more than seeker magic,' said Xing. 'First, we will need to locate where her bones might be.'

'Will that place even exist any more, seeing as the Dragon Realm is falling into the Human Realm?' Dylan pointed out.

'We'll have to hurry,' said Buttons. 'Before the Dragon Realm no longer exists at all.'

'And how are we going to get out of the den when it's surrounded by angry Dragons of Dawn who want to fight us?' said Jordan.

'We don't leave the den at all,' said Billy, grinning up at Spark. 'We make a portal from inside it.'

'So, let me make sure I understand what we're doing,' said Dylan. 'We're going to create a portal to take us to a realm that's falling into our own world, try to locate the bones of an ancient dragon, summon that dragon's spirit and convince her to show us a new realm?'

'Exactly!' said Buttons, sounding delighted.

'You will not have much time in the Dragon Realm,' said Lightning. 'More and more of it is falling into this realm every day.'

'Luckily, when we're there, time works differently,' said Billy. 'Right? So ideally we go in, out, and be back before anything else disastrous happens here.'

'As always, I admire your optimism,' said Dylan.

'Of course there is a chance that the place where Glorious Old's bones are located has already fallen into this realm,' said Tank. 'So we must go quickly to where we suspect they are most likely to be.'

'Where do we even start?' said Lola.

Spark began to crackle with electricity and power, and despite everything, Billy felt a thrum of excitement buzz through him.

'We start with where the legend ends,' said Spark. 'We start with the Cave of Secrets.'

What Makes A Superhero

'You're going to make a portal that takes us straight to the Cave of Secrets?' asked Billy, eyes wide. 'Can you do that?'

'I would if I could,' said Spark. 'But while I have grown much more adept at creating portals, the Cave of Secrets is a hidden and protected place. We cannot take a portal directly there.'

'In which case, we aren't technically starting where the legend ends,' said Dylan. 'So where are we going first?'

Xing whacked him on the behind with her tail. Dylan let out a squawk. 'Must you always be so disrespectful?'

'Sorry, sorry,' mumbled Dylan, rubbing his backside with a grimace. 'But, seriously, where are we going?'

Spark's eyes lit up. 'Dragon Mountain, of course. To gather what we need before we search for Glorious Old.'

'Including our super-suits!' said Ling-Fei. 'Oh, I've missed them!'

'And we can just pop into Dragon Mountain from here in the den?' said Lola, sounding sceptical. 'I thought you guys said the entrance to Dragon Mountain was in China?'

'Portal magic!' said Charlotte. 'I hate travelling by portal, but I can't deny how useful it is.'

'I suppose one benefit of the Dragon Realm collapsing into the Human Realm is that it makes it easier for us to travel between the realms,' mused Buttons. 'The veil between the two is so thin now that magic is seeping everywhere.'

'I just hope there's a Dragon Realm for us to travel to,' said Jordan. 'I still can't believe an entire mountain collapsed from the sky onto Hampstead Heath!'

'Correction – it nearly collapsed,' said Billy with a grin. 'We stopped it, remember?'

'But who's going to stop that kind of thing from happening while we're gone?' said Lola.

'Time works differently in the Dragon Realm,' said Charlotte. 'Barely any time will pass in our world while we're there searching for Glorious Old and the Hidden Realm.'

Jordan let out a low whistle. 'A lot sure is riding on wibbly-wobbly time differences.' He rubbed the back of his neck. 'I should probably tell my mum that I'm going back into the Dragon Realm, shouldn't I?'

'Maybe Jordan's mum can tell all our families?' said Dylan hopefully. 'Although, honestly with everything going on right now, there's no way we can update our families every time we need to save the world.' When nobody replied, Dylan cracked a smile. 'Guys, I'm joking. Surely this is the last time, right?'

'I don't know about that,' said Billy seriously. Things were different now. There was a weight of responsibility resting on his shoulders that he'd never felt before. He wouldn't change anything about the summer with his friends and their dragons, but right now, in this very moment, it was scary how much the world was depending on them. 'This is kind of becoming our thing, isn't it? And with the entirety of the Dragon Realm falling into the Human Realm . . . Well, it looks as if we're needed now more than ever.'

'That makes us sound like superheroes,' said Dylan with another laugh.

'Well, aren't we?' said Charlotte, hands on her hips. 'We've got magic powers and dragons.'

'And special suits!' added Ling-Fei. 'Don't forget about those.'

'I still need a super-suit of my own,' said Jordan.

'Me too,' said Lola.

'We'll make sure you all have protective suits before we go searching for the Cave of Secrets,' promised Buttons.

It didn't take long for Spark and Lightning to make a portal. They both focused their energy on the underwater lake until it was swirling and crackling with power. When they were done, the group gathered around.

'Go now, before things get any worse. We are all counting on you,' said Lightning. Goldie squeaked in agreement and settled on Lightning's head. 'If we need you, we will send Goldie through the portal. It will be able to find you.'

'That is one useful pig,' said Jordan.

'Goldie is no ordinary pig,' said Billy proudly.

'Enough about the pig,' said Xing. 'It is time.'

Even though Billy had been through portals many times, he still hadn't got used to how strange it felt. As they jumped into the swirling portal in the den's lake, he closed his eyes instinctively. Then came the tingling sensation, followed by the feeling that all the air was being pulled from his lungs. Suddenly, he and Spark were back in the great cavern of Dragon Mountain, coming out of a very similar underground lake to the one they had just jumped into.

As Midnight and Jordan burst through the portal, Billy saw Midnight gaze longingly back at the lake, as if she hoped her parents had changed their minds and decided to join the search party. But the portal closed with a *swoosh* as soon as the others had arrived, and it instantly became a lake once more.

'First things first,' said Buttons. 'Let's find your super-suits and make new ones for Jordan and Lola.'

Billy, Dylan, Charlotte and Ling-Fei found their

super-suits where they'd left them. Billy's was blue and black, and as he put it on, he felt it stretch and fit perfectly to his frame, just as it always did. It was made out of magical fabric enhanced with dragon powers, and he knew from experience it could withstand flame, frost and even electric shocks. It was lightweight, almost like a second skin, and with it on, Billy felt invincible.

'I've missed wearing this,' said Charlotte, twirling around in her red super-suit, making the skirt fan out over the trousers. She'd requested a skirt 'for added style' and pockets too. Charlotte was the toughest person Billy had ever met, but according to her, she still wanted to look fabulous while kicking butt.

'I know what you mean,' said Ling-Fei, grinning as she twirled in her own suit. Her silver suit had a high collar, and she looked almost futuristic in it, as if she'd travelled back in time to help them with their mission. 'Now we're ready for whatever comes our way.'

'It's nice to know that if the Dragons of Dawn do manage to track us down, we'll at least be a little more protected,' added Dylan. His super-suit was green, almost the exact shade of Buttons's scales. His glasses glinted in the dim light. They'd been enhanced not to break or even fall off, which was very useful for when they were flying through the sky at breakneck speed.

'You guys are right – these suits are amazing!' said Lola from the end of the cavern where Xing and Spark were fashioning her own super-suit. It was turquoise, like Neptune's scales, and Xing had added some ridges down the back and the arms, almost as if she had scales herself. 'I'm never going to want to take mine off!'

Jordan's suit was created last. It was deep blue and black, and shot through with silver to match his dragon, Midnight. As the fabric stretched and changed shape around him, he grinned at them all. 'This is mad cool,' he said. 'Better than anything that TURBO could come up with.'

'Do not underestimate TURBO,' said Xing. 'Whatever they used to trap both Flame and Neptune was powered with magic from this realm. Frank Albert must have figured out a way to channel magic from here into TURBO technology before he disappeared into the In-Between.'

Billy suddenly felt overwhelmed thinking about how much they were dealing with. TURBO, the Dragons of Dawn, kidnapped world leaders, not to mention the continual collapsing of the Dragon Realm ... Peace between humans and dragons definitely didn't look like an option any more, but what would they do if this new plan to find the Hidden Realm didn't work either?

Spark must have sensed Billy's feelings because he heard her voice in his head. *One step at a time, Billy. Your plan to find Glorious Old is a good one.*

Billy felt the familiar rush of hope and confidence that came from knowing he had Spark by his side, no matter what. He nodded at her in thanks, then looked at his friends.

'Everything has changed,' he said. 'The world as we know it is no longer there, and the Dragon Realm world is disappearing entirely. We have to adapt. We have to be brave. And we have to lead others, because we know more about this world than anyone else.'

'I love it when you do a rousing speech that nobody asked you to do,' said Dylan with a laugh.

Billy flushed but kept talking. 'It's true! Finding

Glorious Old is only the first step in a very big plan. Even if we succeed—'

'And we will,' interrupted Charlotte. 'Also, I like your speeches.' She grinned at him.

'Thanks, Charlotte,' said Billy. 'Anyway, as I was saying, even if we find Glorious Old and the Hidden Realm, we still need to convince the dragons that they'll be happier there. And we still have to deal with everything else happening in our world.'

'We can do it,' said Ling-Fei.

'For sure,' added Lola. 'Especially now that you've got me and Jordan on your team.'

'Too right,' said Jordan.

Billy looked at each of his friends and then up at their dragons. 'Well then, let's go find Glorious Old and save the world one more time.'

The Sinking Forest

As they burst out of Dragon Mountain and into the Dragon Realm, Billy couldn't believe how different it looked. The three moons still sat high in the sky, much to Billy's relief – he didn't know what would happen if an entire moon collapsed into the Human Realm – but the landscape had changed entirely. Mountain ranges that he'd grown used to seeing were completely gone. The familiar peach trees that had dotted the ground were still there, but there weren't nearly as many as before. And he didn't see a sign of dragons anywhere. It felt strange to be in the Dragon Realm, but not see any dragons.

'Where is this Cave of Secrets meant to be?' he called out to Spark.

'Legend says the cave is deep in the Sinking Forest, so we will go there first,' said Spark.

'If we can find it,' added Buttons.

'Wait,' said Dylan, his voice high with panic. 'Have any of you been to this Cave of Secrets before?'

'It is not a place dragons venture,' said Tank.

'And what exactly do you mean by "sinking"?' added Lola. 'That sounds . . . alarming. Is it under the sea?'

'The Sinking Forest is in a sinking valley,' said Buttons. 'The trees grow faster than the ground beneath them sinks.'

'The Dragon Realm is always full of surprises,' said Ling-Fei.

'That's one way of putting it,' said Charlotte. 'When we're in this Sinking Forest, I'm guessing we'll have to watch out for soft spots that could possibly pull us back into the Human Realm, as well as squishy sinking spots that could pull us . . . into the ground?'

'Precisely!' said Buttons, beaming. 'Well done.'

Charlotte curtsied. 'I'm good at figuring things out.'

'So our plan is to find the Sinking Forest, avoid soft and sinking spots, go into the Cave of Secrets and hope that Glorious Old's bones are in there,' said Billy with as much confidence as he could muster.

'As far as plans go, it isn't the worst one we've ever had,' said Dylan. 'At least we'll have our dragons with us.' He turned to Buttons. 'And you know about some of the secrets in this cave, right?'

'Alas, no,' admitted Buttons. 'And unfortunately we won't be able to go into the cave with you. It's where Glorious Old lived when she was still alive, and she enchanted the cave so no other dragons could enter.'

'But didn't a human kill her?' asked Lola. 'Why was she afraid of dragons?'

'It was not fear that made her enchant the cave against other dragons. She did it to protect her hoard,' said Tank.

'Why didn't she also enchant it against humans?' asked Billy.

'Before Glorious Old was slain, dragons had no reason to fear humans. She would not have thought to keep humans out,' answered Tank.

'We still have no reason to fear humans,' muttered Xing.

'You do, whether you want to or not,' said Lola.

'We've all seen what humans are capable of, especially with TURBO technology at their fingertips.'

'After Glorious Old was slain, peace between humans and dragons became a distant dream,' said Spark. 'Dragons wanted revenge, and humans knew that dragons could be killed. The realms became more divided than ever, and the entrances between the two became harder and harder to find. In ancient times, humans and dragons used to go between the realms more frequently.'

'Of course, not all dragons and humans became enemies,' said Buttons. 'Some were still heart-bonded – the heart bond has always been the most powerful thing in both realms. But it became harder for dragons to find humans who had hearts that matched their own. Humans could no longer be trusted.'

'The funny thing is,' said Neptune, who had been quiet for most of this conversation, 'supposedly Glorious Old loved humans. She was kind to them and tried to help any who found themselves in the Dragon Realm . . . until they betrayed her.'

Lola leaned over and stroked Neptune on her head. 'I'd never betray you,' she promised.

'Humans can be good!' chimed in Midnight. 'Our humans are proof of that!'

'Exactly,' said Spark. 'And our humans will save us all.'

'If we can find those bones,' said Dylan. 'It's a pretty big if.'

'If anyone can, we can,' said Billy confidently. He glanced over at Ling-Fei and grinned at his friend. 'Especially with Ling-Fei and Xing leading the way.'

'You humans are lucky I like you all so much,' said Xing. 'Come, Ling-Fei. Together we can use our powers to seek out the Sinking Forest.'

They took off into the sky, even Neptune, who looked like a flying submarine, and Billy felt the familiar jolt of joy that came from flying on his dragon in the Dragon Realm.

As they flew, parts of the realm disappeared before their eyes. Most of the time it was something small, like a tree or a boulder, but once, one of the floating islands in front of them simply slipped out of the sky.

Billy's stomach lurched as he realized that the soft spots where the Dragon Realm was falling into the Human Realm were everywhere. Not just on the ground, but in the sky and the seas too. They could fly into a soft spot and have no idea until it was too late.

'How long do you think it will take for the entire Dragon Realm to fall into the Human Realm?' he asked Spark.

She was quiet for a moment. 'It is hard to say. And as you know, time works differently here, which means it might happen quickly in your realm and slower in ours. But it is happening quickly enough that staying here is no longer an option for dragons.' She sighed deeply. 'I hope that the Hidden Realm is suitable.'

'Me too.'

On and on they flew, the sky changing from brilliant blue to dusty lavender and finally dark indigo. As the twinkling stars shone above, Billy had another thought.

'What about all the stars? The stars that used to be dragons? Will they come into the Human Realm?'

'Eventually, yes,' said Spark. 'Although I imagine

some of the stars we see here are ones you can already see in your realm.'

Billy liked the idea that some of the stars he'd grown up seeing were the same ones that the dragons had seen; that some of them were the spirits of dragons from long ago.

As they continued on their journey, they didn't see any other living dragons. Either they were all hiding or they'd already fallen into the Human Realm. It was too much for Billy to think about.

He stayed looking ahead towards the horizon, trying to spot where the Sinking Forest might be, and suddenly thought he saw an eye looking back at him from the sky. He blinked, and then it was gone. He was getting tired, and he wasn't the only one. Charlotte let out a ginormous yawn, and Dylan took off his glasses to rub his eyes.

'I'm exhausted,' announced Lola.

'Me too,' said Jordan. 'I don't even remember the last time I slept.'

'It feels like a long, long, long time ago,' said Dylan as he put his glasses back on.

'We should rest,' said Tank. 'The children need sleep.'

'We can do what we've done before,' said Buttons. 'We can fly on while they sleep on our backs.'

'What if you find the Sinking Forest during the night?' asked Billy with a yawn of his own.

'We will wake you,' said Xing in her typical 'isn't it obvious' tone.

'Do not worry,' added Spark more gently. 'Sleep while you can.'

Billy leaned forward and rested his head on his dragon's neck, letting the sound of her beating wings lull him to sleep.

For a brief moment, when Billy woke, he forgot where he was.

The wind blew gently around his face and the rising sun cast a golden glow over his surroundings. Then everything came back in a rush. The disastrous meeting with the world leaders, the Dragons of Dawn, TURBO, the Thunder Clan den on the heath and their arrival in the Dragon Realm with the hopes of finding the bones of a dead dragon and convincing her spirit to show them the way to a new realm.

Billy let out a long breath. He couldn't lose faith,

not in the plan, not in his friends, not in himself. He had to stay focused and hopeful, and he reminded himself of everything else they'd faced before. But still . . . this felt like their greatest challenge yet. If the most powerful humans in the world didn't know how to handle this, how were he and his friends meant to?

Billy? Spark's voice echoed in his head. *Are you feeling okay? I can sense some . . . anxiousness from you.*

Their connection meant that not only could they speak down their bond, but Spark could sense how Billy was feeling. She always knew the right moment to reassure him.

It's all just a lot to deal with, Billy thought back. *What if we can't do it?*

I know, Spark answered. *But there is no way to go but forward.*

What if we don't find Glorious Old? Billy would have never voiced the fear out loud, especially not around his friends, but he was grateful to be able to let Spark know how he was really feeling; grateful he didn't need to keep his worries to himself.

Then we will come up with another plan. But do not anticipate failure until it has happened. Otherwise, you will become paralysed by the fear of it potentially going wrong. Hope is a powerful force, Billy.

Thank you, Spark, Billy thought back. *I needed that.*

Spark was right. He had to stay positive. He squinted into the distance, trying to see if he could spot anything that might guide them towards the Sinking Forest.

Xing flew slightly ahead of Spark, and Ling-Fei suddenly sat bolt upright on her back. 'There!' she cried, pointing. 'That must be it!'

'I can't see anything,' said Jordan with a yawn. He had woken up a few moments before on Midnight's back.

'That dark shadow,' said Ling-Fei. 'Just beyond the river. That's it. That's the Sinking Forest!'

'How do you know?' said Charlotte.

Ling-Fei sat up even straighter, straining forward as if she could hear music none of the others could. 'Because it's calling out to me. It's been waiting for us.'

The Cave Of Secrets

Even though Billy was used to Ling-Fei being able to hear nature in a way that nobody else could, he still couldn't quite comprehend what she was saying. It wasn't that he didn't believe her – after all, he'd once seen her speak to a mountain and convince it to carry them – he knew she was telling the truth. He just struggled to process the fact that the forest was apparently calling out to them; waiting for them.

'What do you mean, the forest has been waiting for us?' Billy said as they flew closer and closer to the shadowy shape by the edge of the horizon. As they approached it, he began to see the outlines of the trees that made up the forest. There were hundreds of them, each one stretching up high towards the sky. And they were all growing out of what looked like a natural basin in the ground. The Sinking Forest.

'I can't explain it exactly,' said Ling-Fei, her brow furrowing as she concentrated on the sound that only she could hear. 'But either the forest itself or something in it is calling us. It's expecting us.'

'Maybe it's the Cave of Secrets itself!' squealed Midnight.

'Perhaps,' said Xing. 'Very little is known about the Cave of Secrets.'

'I hope it isn't a trap,' said Jordan uneasily.

'Ling-Fei would know if it was a trap,' said Billy. 'Right? You'd be able to tell.'

Ling-Fei closed her eyes for a long moment. 'I can't tell if the voice is nice or not, just that it's coming from the Sinking Forest.'

Billy gulped. 'Well, hopefully whatever we find there will be nice and will be happy to help us find Glorious Old.'

They flew in closer, until they were right at the edge of the forest. This close, Billy could see that the ground underneath the trees was spongy. He even saw one tree begin to sink, a huge chunk disappearing into the ground with a *swoosh* faster than he'd expected. But the tree was so tall that it still climbed into the sky, even as its roots were swallowed up by the ground below.

He wanted to stay on his dragon in the air to avoid sinking into the forest floor too, but the trees were too dense and close together for the dragons to keep flying. They'd have to go by foot. Only Xing was able to stay in the air, winding her way through the trees like a wisp of smoke, but Ling-Fei walked.

'Do you know what I dislike even more than flying?' said Neptune as they all began to make their way into the forest. 'Walking. Dragons are not made to walk. We are made to fly in the air or the water, not walk through soggy-bottomed forests.'

Lola burst out laughing. 'Oh, Neptune, don't be so grouchy,' she said affectionately. 'We'll only be in here for a little while. We just need to find the Cave of Secrets and then we'll get out of here. We'll have you back in the sea in no time.'

'Are we sure there's a cave here at all? All I see are trees,' said Jordan. 'Trees and trees and –' he lifted his foot up with some effort – 'this muck.'

'The cave is here,' said Spark. 'The old stories all say that the Cave of Secrets, where Glorious Old resided, is in the Sinking Forest.'

'Ah, yes, the old stories – what a trustworthy source of information,' said Dylan. 'Why can't we ever have a map?'

'Dragons don't use maps. What a silly idea,' said Midnight with a laugh. 'We all have an excellent sense of direction, and the stories are the best thing to guide us! I still can't believe that Glorious Old is real!'

'Anyway, a map would be useless now that things are all moving and disappearing,' added Tank. 'It is lucky we found the Sinking Forest, and we should move quickly to find the cave.'

'What if the cave is already in the Human Realm?' said Billy, feeling overwhelmed at the mere possibility that the cave, and the bones, could be anywhere in either realm.

'We will find out soon enough,' said Spark. 'And, remember, when we find the entrance to the cave, only the six of you can go in. Glorious Old enchanted the cave to stop any other dragons entering.'

'Remind me why she did that again?' asked

Charlotte, nimbly hopping over a particularly menacing-looking thorn bush.

'The same reason any dragon hides the entrance to their home – to protect their hoard from other dragons. That was the only thing dragons worried about during the time of Glorious Old,' said Tank. 'But after she was slain, dragons grew more violent – towards each other and towards humans.'

'You see, Glorious Old was a keeper of peace,' said Spark, bowing her head with reverence, as if the dragon could see her. Then she looked up, eyes sparkling. 'But, of course, even peaceful dragons want to protect their hoards.'

Xing zoomed round a tree so she was facing the children. She grinned at them all. 'If you see any good treasure in that cave, make sure to bring it out to us. I do love treasure! And Glorious Old has no need for it now.'

'Xing!' chided Ling-Fei. 'That isn't very respectful.'

Xing sighed. 'Fine. Focus on finding her bones. I suppose that is the important part.'

They carried on through the forest, careful not to get too close to any trees that looked as if they were sinking faster than the others.

'I'm starting to think the stories are false. There's no cave here,' said Lola, looking up towards the sky. 'All I see are these giant trees.'

Billy craned his neck, trying to spot the tops of the trees, but they stretched into the clouds.

Dylan looked up too, squinting behind his glasses. 'Do you think the cave is at the top of one of these trees? Like a *Jack and the Beanstalk* situation?'

Jordan scrunched up his face. 'The trees look too close together for us to fly there and check it out, and there's no way I'm climbing *all* the way up one of those trunks.'

'Nonsense,' said Tank, shaking his head. 'No cave is in the sky.'

'I mean, we literally rode a walking cave in the sky a few months ago,' said Dylan.

'And entire mountain ranges have been falling from the sky in the Human Realm,' added Lola.

Tank let out a huff but didn't argue.

Xing continued weaving through the trees around them, her eyes glowing gold. 'I am sure that the cave's entrance is near. I can sense it. It feels too close to be somewhere up in the sky.'

'I agree,' said Ling-Fei, her face serious. 'Let me see if I can locate it. I'll use our bond to boost my senses.' She closed her eyes and brought her fingers to her temples. She was quiet for a moment as she swivelled her head slowly from side to side, like a searchlight in the dark. Her head moved in a wide semicircle at first, turning from shoulder to shoulder, but gradually it slowed down until she was facing a single tree. Her eyes popped open and she walked up to it, placing a hand on its rough bark. 'This one,' said Ling-Fei with a smile. 'And the entrance isn't at the top of this tree, but *under* it.'

On closer inspection, Billy could see that the tree was much thicker than the other trees around them.

'Very well done, Ling-Fei,' said Xing, who couldn't hide her smile. 'Your abilities have grown much stronger.'

'I will take care of this,' said Tank as he strode forward. 'Stand back.'

He squatted down at the base of the tree, digging his hind claws into the earth. Then he clamped his jaws around the tree, opened his wings wide and flapped so hard Billy had to shield his eyes from the dirt flying everywhere. The tree shuddered and the ground rumbled as it started to shake free from its place in the ground. Tank let out a loud roar through gritted teeth, pulling and pushing with all his might. The tree rose a few centimetres, looking as if it might release its hold on the earth, before it sprang back into the ground.

'This is no ordinary tree,' said Xing, a hint of amusement in her voice as she watched Tank furiously trying to unearth it.

Spark swooped up into the air and gripped the tree with her claws, beating her wings furiously above Tank. The tree inched up further, bit by bit, before it finally released its grip on the earth with a *pop*.

Billy was surprised to see that the tree didn't have any roots. Instead, it lifted out of the ground as if it were a lid on a pot, revealing a dark black pool of liquid.

'Watch where you swing that thing,' quipped Xing, moving away from the now loose tree.

Billy stared into the black pool in front of him, his shadowy reflection staring back. He couldn't tell how deep the water was, but the liquid was so slick and such a deep shade of black that it looked as if it could be a bottomless pit of oil. He wondered whether anything was lurking beneath the shimmering surface. What kind of creatures would even be able to survive in such a place?

'If that's the entrance, count me out,' said Jordan, taking a step back.

'I fear it is the only way,' said Spark.

'So are we meant to just jump into this black pit and hope we can somehow feel our way to the entrance to the cave?' said Lola.

Dylan examined the pool closer. 'I don't know if we'll even be able to move in that stuff. It looks about as easy as swimming in a giant tub of tar.'

Ling-Fei walked towards the edge of the pool and leaned down to inspect it more closely.

Billy held his breath, half expecting something to spring out of the liquid and swallow her whole.

'You look like a friendly pool,' Ling-Fei said in her sing-song voice. After studying it for a few moments, she dipped a fingertip into the liquid.

The pool began to swirl and a tendril of black liquid shot out and wrapped round Ling-Fei's wrist.

Then another emerged and twisted round her waist. Ling-Fei screamed and, in the next instant, two more tendrils took hold of each ankle. Before Billy had even taken a step towards her, more black tendrils shot out of the pool, soon covering Ling-Fei entirely. Billy blinked, hardly believing what he was seeing, and then Ling-Fei was gone.

Billy felt as if his heart had stopped. Even with his super speed, the tendrils had shot out and pulled in Ling-Fei so fast that he had only taken two strides by the time she'd been completely pulled under.

'LING-FEI!' Billy cried. 'I'M COMING FOR YOU!'

And without another thought, Billy dived headfirst into the black abyss. He felt as if he were free falling through a starless night sky. Down, down, down he went, as if he were being swallowed deep within the earth like a secret. He thrashed his arms and kicked his legs, trying to orient himself, but he kept sinking.

As he tried to control his panic, Billy felt a thick, slimy rope wrap itself round his wrist like a snake. Then another attached itself to his other wrist. And then both his ankles. In only a few moments, Billy was completely covered from the neck down, and the bands hardened, sealing him in as if he were in a cocoon.

Billy continued to free fall like a rock through the sky until *plop*! He'd landed feet first into something squishy. It cushioned his fall, catching him like a glove. For a fleeting moment, Billy was relieved that *something* had caught him, grateful that his crash landing hadn't gone worse, or that he hadn't been caught in an infinite free fall.

He hoped he was in the Cave of Secrets, but even if he was in the cave, now he was *stuck*. Stuck up to his neck in the ground like a crop ready for harvest. Billy wriggled back and forth, trying to loosen the earth's hold on him, but it was useless. The earth gripped him like an iron fist, its clench tightening the more he struggled.

'Hello? Is someone there?' said a voice Billy recognized.

'Ling-Fei!' Billy replied. 'Are you okay?'

'Er, I guess so. I feel fine. I don't think I hurt anything when I landed. I'm just a bit . . . stuck.'

Just then, Billy heard faint cries above them. They were distant at first but got louder and louder until . . . *Plop! Plop! Plop! Plop!*

'HELLO? Ling-Fei! Billy! Can you hear me?'

'Lola! Is that you?' shouted Billy.

'And me,' said another voice that Billy immediately knew was Charlotte. It was hard to miss her southern drawl she had from growing up in Atlanta.

'Is everyone here?' said Billy, surprised.

'That was wild,' said Jordan.

'I'm here too,' replied Dylan.

'You shouldn't all have come!' cried Ling-Fei.

'Of course we were going to come after you. We're a team,' answered Lola.

'What even is this place?' said Charlotte.

Billy waited for his eyes to adjust to the dark of the cave. He could just about make out the faces of each of his friends, all of whom were stuck neck-deep in the ground.

'This is bad,' said Dylan.

Charlotte turned her head towards Dylan. 'Could you be any more obvious with your observations?'

'Well,' said Dylan, 'I think we should get out of here.'

'Thanks again, Captain Obvious,' said Charlotte, rolling her eyes, but Billy could tell she was smiling.

'*Hrrmph!*'

Billy looked over his shoulder and saw Lola's face screwed up in effort as she wriggled and wriggled, trying to break free. 'I don't think I could be any more stuck if I tried,' she said.

'I think I can break my way out,' said Charlotte with a grunt as she rocked back and forth. She was so strong that her movements made the entire ground around them shake. 'Nearly there,' she said, and then she sank down completely into the earth, head too.

'That is . . . the opposite of getting out,' said Dylan.

'Charlotte!' yelled Billy.

There was a moment of silence and then Charlotte popped up and out of the ground, scattering dirt everywhere. 'Ah-ha! I had to go under to get enough leverage to burst out!' she said, sounding triumphant. 'It just needed a bit of muscle!' Then she started brushing the dirt off her skirt.

She'd managed to break out of the cocoon, but the black tar-like substance had left a coat of ash all over her clothes. Draped in all black, it almost looked as if she was wearing a wet suit, similar to the ones Billy wore when he went surfing back in California. And for a fleeting moment, he wondered whether he'd ever go surfing again. He pushed the thought from his mind.

'When you're done cleaning yourself off,' said Dylan, 'would you mind helping out those of us who aren't outrageously strong?'

'At your service,' Charlotte replied with a curtsey. She walked over to Lola, careful not to kick dirt into her face, and plunged her arms into the ground. 'Ladies first.'

Billy felt the earth tremble again as Charlotte stirred her arms in circles, loosening the soil.

Lola beamed. 'It's working! It's working!'

Then Charlotte knelt close to Lola and hoisted her up. Lola was out of the earth, but her whole body was still in a cocoon of dirt. Charlotte laid her down and raised a clenched fist above her. 'Brace yourself,' she said, and she brought her fist down onto Lola's chest like a hammer. Lola winced as the cocoon shattered around her, then opened one eye tentatively.

'You're welcome,' Charlotte said, picking up Lola and setting her on her feet as if she were a doll.

Lola held out her arms and legs, checking to see if they were all still there. 'I swear you stopped my heart for a split second, but thank you.'

'Me next,' said Dylan. 'But less dramatic, please.'

One by one, Charlotte helped free all her friends by loosening the earth's grip and hammering them out of their shells.

'Who needs a sledgehammer when you have Charlotte's fists?' said Dylan.

'My thoughts exactly,' said Jordan, throwing an arm round Charlotte's shoulders.

'Yeah, we'll definitely be able to defend ourselves if we do come across anything in the cave,' said Lola with a grin. 'That was so impressive!'

'I do what I can,' said Charlotte, dusting off her hands. 'Now, let's get back to finding those bones.'

Billy gave Charlotte a quick high five and then turned to Ling-Fei. 'What are your senses telling you, Ling-Fei?' he said. 'Any ancient dragon bones around?'

Ling-Fei closed her eyes again, but before she'd

even managed to bring her fingers to her temples, her eyes shot open. '*Something's coming. And fast.*' She pointed to the left, but it was so dark in the cave that Billy couldn't make out anything past their group.

'Everyone stand back to back,' said Jordan. 'So nothing can sneak up on us.'

The group formed a tight circle, standing shoulder to shoulder, their backs facing in.

'What's the plan?' said Dylan.

But before anyone could respond, a faint glow emerged from the direction where Ling-Fei had pointed. In the distance, it looked like a ball made up of a thousand neon fireflies, each one a different colour and all of them dazzling. As it drew closer, Billy saw that it was a bird, with huge wings that arched like boomerangs. It drew nearer still and he realized it looked like a crane made purely of light, leaving a fluorescent rainbow trail in its wake as it flew.

'It's beautiful,' said Ling-Fei. 'I sense that this crane is good at heart.'

'Well, we're going to find out soon enough,' said Lola.

The crane made of light swooped down in front

of them, stretching its neck from left to right as it studied the group.

'We welcome you, crane,' said Ling-Fei.

The crane walked up to Ling-Fei on its slender legs, examining her with its black, beady eyes. It leaned forward, its nose nearly touching Ling-Fei's, but Ling-Fei didn't flinch. She stared straight back into the bird's eyes. The crane paused for a moment, before straightening up, its dark eyes still fixed on Ling-Fei. It stretched its wings out, flapped them a couple of times and let out a high-pitched caw.

Dylan held back a scream as the crane lifted back into the air and circled above them, leaving a ring of sparkling light, before flying back in the direction it came from.

'Well, that seemed kind of pointless,' said Dylan.

'Look at us,' said Billy, holding up his hands.

What had previously looked like black ash on their clothes was now alight and alive with colour. The six of them lit up the cave like candles in the dark, all of them glowing a hundred shades of neon.

'At least we can see now,' said Jordan.

'Maybe we can find a way out,' said Dylan.

'We need to get Glorious Old's bones first!' said Charlotte. 'I didn't fall all this way to go back empty-handed.'

'She's right,' said Lola. 'We need those bones.'

'I think we need to follow that crane,' said Ling-Fei. 'It wants us to go after it.'

'How do we know we can trust it? What if it's a trap?' said Dylan anxiously.

Billy looked around in the new light. They were at a crossroads in the cave system – he counted at least six different paths they could take. 'I think following the crane is our best option. I know it might be a trap, but that's a risk we're going to have to take. Who knows what could be down the other paths?'

'Billy's right,' said Lola. 'We should trust Ling-Fei's instincts. It's the best map we have.'

'Good enough for me,' said Dylan.

'All right,' said Jordan. 'Let's go.'

'I'll lead the way,' said Charlotte. 'And if anything jumps out at us, I'll punch it on the nose.'

The path the crane had taken led deeper into the belly of the earth, and the group trod carefully to avoid slipping. After a while, Billy realized that the cave was getting brighter the deeper they went. While the walls were pitch-black at the cave entrance, they were now emitting a soft pink and blue light. They went round bends and through pools, but always down and deeper into the earth. As they trekked, the path got narrower and the ceiling shorter. Large stone spikes jutted out of the floor and down from the ceiling like terrible teeth.

'We're close,' said Ling-Fei as they rounded a corner.

The path ahead of them was so bright, Billy had to shield his eyes. The walls of the cave were still glowing, but even brighter than that were the piles upon piles of jewels and gemstones. Diamonds as big as watermelons sparkled as if they were stars in the sky.

'This must be it! This must be Glorious Old's hoard,' said Charlotte with excitement.

'Yes! We did it! Now we just have to find her bones . . .' added Lola.

'Well, it was mostly Ling-Fei and Charlotte, but I guess we could call it a team effort,' said Dylan.

'And look!' cried Jordan. 'The crane is back!'

The crane had appeared again from deeper within

the cave, its glowing brilliance one of the most spectacular things Billy had ever seen. He was almost mesmerized as it circled the hoard, deftly manoeuvring between the spikes jutting out from the floor and ceiling. It spun and swooped around the cave, leaving a beautiful trail of light behind it. The bird had flown three times round the room when it suddenly shot into a small opening in the path next to them. If it wasn't for the crane, Billy would have missed it.

'Follow that bird!' said Billy. 'I bet it's leading us to Glorious Old's bones.'

The group ran after the crane and into the opening. It led to an even smaller space, except one with more spikes and no jewels.

Dylan was the last to enter the space through the gap, and as soon as he did, a solid rock slab fell from the top of the opening, sealing them in. They all gasped, and Lola let out a small shriek. They were trapped.

The crane that had led them into the space turned to face them. Billy could have sworn it flashed them a smile before it vanished, leaving nothing but a trail of shimmering light behind.

It was then that the cave started to move. The ground shook all around them, so hard Billy thought his legs might give out.

'Er, guys,' said Dylan anxiously. 'Is it just me, or is the cave closing in on us?'

'Oh, I really hope it's just you,' said Lola. But Billy could see that the ceiling was definitely starting to move down.

'The cave is going to eat us!' cried Dylan.

'Don't be ridiculous, Dylan,' said Charlotte, flipping her hair over her shoulder. 'No cave is going to eat us. Not if I can help it.'

Charlotte ran over to a raised section of the space and reached her hands above her. From where she was standing, the ceiling had lowered enough for her to touch the top of the cave.

Billy gasped. 'Charlotte, be careful!'

Charlotte gritted her teeth as she pushed with all her might against the cave ceiling. The whole room buckled and huge cracks split the walls as she held it up.

'I ... don't ... know ... how ... long ... I ... can ... hold ... this ... for,' she said with a grunt.

A deep croaking echoed through the room, as if the cave were laughing at them, or perhaps it was the crane.

'Honourable crane,' Ling-Fei cried. 'I know you can hear us. And I know you are good.'

'Thieves have been caught!' The words whooshed around them, as if they were flying on silent wings. 'Thieves came to steal my master's jewels! Now the cave will grind the thieves to dust!'

'That sounds deeply unpleasant,' said Dylan.

'Please, honourable crane, we're not thieves,' said Ling-Fei. 'We've come to find your master's bones. We want to summon her.'

'We seek Glorious Old!' said Billy. 'We need her help.'

'Humans harmed my master. Humans must not be trusted,' said the voice, and then light illuminated a corner of the room, and Billy realized it was the voice of the crane. The crane itself was made of light.

'Please, honourable crane,' said Billy. There was a creak as the ceiling of the cave moved down even lower.

'I can't hold it much longer!' yelled Charlotte.

'Dylan, can't you try to convince it? That's your skill, isn't it?'

'Oh, well remembered!' said Dylan. He cleared his throat. 'Honourable crane, glorious creature, we speak the truth. We are pure of heart. We have bonded with dragons and we want to help them. We can only do that if we summon Glorious Old.'

There was a flicker of light as the crane grew more solid again. It flew close to Dylan's face, peering at him carefully, and then let out a squawk. 'You may be speaking words to charm me, but they are not false words. I can tell.' It looked at each of them in turn, and to Billy's astonishment, a fat tear rolled down its cheek. 'I would help you if I could, but my master's bones are not here. She did not return to the Cave of Secrets to die.' Billy felt his heart sink, but the crane kept speaking.

'But even if I cannot help you find my master's bones, I can stop you from having your bones crushed. HALT!'

The cave did as it was commanded and stopped moving. Charlotte collapsed to the floor, her face red and sweaty. 'About time,' she heaved. 'A minute later and we would have been toast.'

'Honourable crane, we thank you for saving us, but surely you must know where your master went?' said Ling-Fei.

'Also, if we're asking for favours, can the crane help us get out of here?' added Jordan.

'My glorious master, Glorious Old, the first dragon and the best dragon, went back home. To her first home,' spoke the crane.

'And where is that?' said Billy.

But the crane was no longer listening. 'You will be spat out where you came from,' it said, eyes glowing brightly. 'Goodbye.'

'Wait!' cried Billy. 'Where was her first home?'

But the cave was already rumbling to life again, and it was suddenly filled with the same oily liquid that had dragged them down. It was pouring out from cracks and crevices in the cave walls, but this time it sent them back up into the light.

They landed in a heap at the feet of their dragons.

Xing blinked down at them. 'I take it you did not find the bones.'

The Crimson Volcano

'The glowing crane told us that Glorious Old had gone back home,' said Billy. 'But I thought her home was her cave?'

'It was not her first home,' said Spark suddenly. 'Oh, I should have remembered the story better. Glorious Old was born in a volcano.'

'Whoa,' said Lola, sounding impressed. 'That's gnarly.'

'And not just any volcano,' Spark went on. 'The Crimson Volcano – the most active and unpredictable volcano in all of the Dragon Realm.'

'Now I see why we didn't start by looking in this volcano,' said Dylan.

'Do you think we can trust the crane?' said Jordan. 'It did try to lure us deep into a cave that wanted to swallow us.'

'It had no reason to lie to us,' said Ling-Fei. 'It spoke the truth about Glorious Old.'

'How sure are we that there won't be something waiting in the volcano to devour us?' said Dylan.

'Oh, there most certainly will be something unpleasant in the volcano,' said Buttons. 'You'll just have to outsmart it. But you're all good at that.'

'So where is this Crimson Volcano?' said Billy. 'We need to find it before we can even think about facing whatever unpleasantness is inside it.'

'It was last seen in the Forgotten Sea,' said Tank.

'Oooh, wonderful!' Charlotte brushed off some of the glitter still stuck to her suit. 'I for one wouldn't mind a quick dip in the sea to get all of this stuff off me.'

'I still can't believe we went into the Cave of Secrets for nothing,' said Dylan glumly. 'Nearly swallowed by a cave and we didn't even come close to finding the bones we were looking for.'

'It wasn't for nothing,' said Buttons. 'We'd have

never thought to go to the Crimson Volcano. It may have been Glorious Old's birthplace, but it certainly isn't where I'd have thought to find her bones. One clue leads to the next.'

'I just hope this is the final clue,' said Billy. 'Get to the volcano, find the bones, summon the spirit ...' He trailed off as he realized that even if the Crimson Volcano did hold Glorious Old's bones, it was far from the final step. He sighed and ran his hand through his hair. 'We need *something* to go right,' he said. 'We're running out of time.'

The group flew off towards the Forgotten Sea – a magical sea that only appeared to those who knew of its existence. As they soared over it, Billy breathed in deeply, inhaling the smell of lemons. Underwater citrus trees grew along the sea floor, and it made the whole sea smell amazing.

Using his bond with Spark, Billy guided them down closer to the water itself so he could trail his fingers in it and feel the sea spray on his face. Just being by the sea calmed him. It reminded him of California, of home.

'I'm going in!' cried Charlotte, and with a warrior cry, she leaped off Tank's head and cannonballed into the sea. 'Woo-hoo!' A huge splash went up where she landed, and moments later, her head burst out of the water. 'It feels amazing!'

'We do not have time to play,' said Xing with a sniff.

'I'm just trying to get rid of some of that cave gunk,' said Charlotte, sticking her tongue out at Xing. The silver dragon returned the gesture and it made everyone laugh.

'All right, all right, I'm getting out,' said Charlotte. 'This stuff still won't come off anyway.'

They flew on over the Forgotten Sea, and the longer they travelled over the shining turquoise waters, the tenser they all became.

Then the dragons stopped in mid-air and hovered over a spot in the sea.

'The Crimson Volcano should be here,' said Xing.

'And yet it is not,' said Spark.

Dread curdled in Billy's stomach.

'What do you mean the volcano isn't here?' sputtered Dylan, voicing Billy's alarm.

Spark nodded down at the Forgotten Sea. 'It should be there, and it is not.'

'Oh no – it's fallen into the Human Realm, hasn't it?' said Charlotte in a panic.

'So it seems,' said Spark.

'It could be *anywhere*,' cried Lola. 'Literally anywhere in the whole world.'

'We can track it,' said Ling-Fei. 'We've tracked down things before. We just found that cave, didn't we?'

'And look how that worked out!' said Dylan. 'We nearly got eaten by said cave, all thanks to a tricksy glow-in-the-dark bird!'

'We survived though, didn't we?' said Charlotte.

'What if it's fallen through a soft spot and landed at the bottom of the sea in the Human Realm?' said Jordan. 'How will we be able to find it then?'

Midnight let out an alarmed chirp. 'I can't go to the bottom of the sea!'

'Not a problem,' said Neptune with what Billy could have sworn was a grin, or at least the closest thing he'd seen to a grin on the giant sea dragon's face. 'At least, not a problem for me.'

Billy stared down at the Forgotten Sea. 'If it fell through a soft spot here . . . wouldn't we just need to fall in the same spot?'

'It won't be exact,' said Buttons. 'But it will hopefully bring us close to where the volcano landed.'

'We could land *anywhere*,' said Dylan with a groan. 'We could land in TURBO headquarters! Or, you know, actually in the volcano.'

'In the volcano would be pretty useful,' said Billy. 'Do you think our super-suits could survive it?' He expected the dragons to laugh, but instead they all gazed seriously back at him.

'Not even dragons can survive volcano lava,' said Tank. 'It is no laughing matter.'

'So how exactly are we meant to get our hands on Glorious Old's bones if they're in the volcano?' asked Lola, her eyebrows raised.

'Very, very carefully,' said Neptune. 'Now, you may remember that before I realized our entire realm was crashing into the Human Realm, I was searching for soft spots to figure out what was happening. I do not have Xing's ability to sense magic, but I can sense disturbances in water. And right now, well, I believe there is a soft spot in the Forgotten Sea that the Crimson Volcano fell through.'

Billy looked at his friends and their dragons. 'We

make these decisions together,' he said. 'What do you guys think we should do?'

'I think it's utter madness, but that's never stopped us before,' said Dylan cheerfully.

'We need to find those bones,' said Charlotte. 'And I'm not scared of a volcano.'

'You aren't scared of anything,' said Ling-Fei, laughing. 'But I agree – let's continue our mission.'

'I know I'm new to this team, but I don't give up once I start something,' said Jordan.

'Me neither,' said Lola. 'And I want to make the world safe for both humans and dragons.'

Billy's friends' optimism and confidence buoyed his own. They were right. They could do this. Especially if they were together. He grinned at his friends. 'Then let's do this.'

Billy wasn't sure what falling through a soft spot was going to feel like. He'd gone through portals, entered the In-Between and even fallen through time, so he shouldn't have been nervous, but he was.

As Spark and the other dragons dived down into the sea, with the children on their backs and Neptune leading the way, Billy was surprised that the soft spot wasn't pulling them towards it like a whirlpool. It had no suction at all, and as they went through it, Billy felt as if they were puncturing a bubble. There was a bright flash of gold light, and Billy realized they were suddenly in the In-Between. But it looked completely different from the last time he'd seen it.

'Hold on!' cried Spark. 'Do not fall! There is golden elixir everywhere!'

Before Billy had time to contemplate why that might be, or what it might be doing to the In-Between, or maybe even both realms, they burst through the other side into the Human Realm. They were upside down and spinning with the sea above them and the sky below, and Billy felt the wind get knocked out of him. As Spark righted herself and Billy caught his breath, he began to grin.

There, in the distance, was a bright red volcano, glowing like a beacon in the sea.

The Crimson Volcano. It had to be.

'Where are we?' asked Jordan as they soared over the water towards the volcano. 'It's way too hot for us to be anywhere near England!' He and Midnight were flying right next to Billy and Spark, and on Midnight's other side were Xing and Ling-Fei. Neptune and Lola were in the water below, with Neptune's head above water and Lola gripping tightly to the pointed scales at the back of her head. Tank and Charlotte flew at the back, as usual, and Buttons and Dylan were on Billy and Spark's other side.

'I think we are somewhere in what you call the Pacific Ocean,' said Xing.

'Whoa, how do you know that?' said Jordan, clearly impressed.

'I already told you, Jordan, dragons don't need maps. We always know where we are,' said Midnight.

Billy grinned and shook his head at Midnight's confidence. Then something caught his eye.

The air directly above them was shimmering.

'Something's happening!' he cried out. 'The sky! It's moving!'

'A portal is opening up,' said Xing, her voice laced with panic. 'Quick, quick, get out of the way. Who knows what will come through it!'

'FASTER!' roared Tank.

All the dragons shot through the sky, so fast it made

Billy's teeth rattle. Only when they were far enough from the shimmering spot did he glance back. It was just in time to see around a dozen yellow and orange dragons tumble out of the portal and race after them. Even from this distance, Billy could hear them shouting their strange chant. It sent chills up his spine.

'Looks as if we've got company!' he shouted. 'The Dragons of Dawn are on our tail!'

'I guess they didn't get bored of waiting for us to come out of the den,' said Dylan.

'How did they find us?' cried Charlotte.

'They must have been tracking us somehow,' said Spark.

'We are very powerful all together,' added Xing. 'If any of them have a seeker skill similar to mine, they would have been waiting for an influx of power in the Human Realm to be able to sense where we were. A strong gathering of dragons, such as us, emits an unmistakable aura of power.'

'Whoa,' said Billy. 'Can we mask it?' It made him nervous to know they could be so easily tracked.

'Yes, and we should have thought of that, but it's too late now,' said Buttons.

'Oh! It's like my mum!' said Midnight. 'Remember? The only way for her to hide her power from the Dragon of Death was to be put asleep in our house.'

Billy wished they had Lightning, and her epic power, with them now. At the time, it had made sense for her and Thunder to stay in the Human Realm to keep an eye on things, but now that they were back there, he wished they were with them. He glanced at Midnight, who was staring resolutely ahead as she flew. He had a feeling she too wished her parents were with them.

'Luckily, the Dragons of Dawn do not seem to be as fast as us,' said Xing smugly. 'We will reach the volcano before they catch us.'

The volcano rose up ahead of them, smoking ominously. It jutted out of the sea like a giant crooked tooth. Billy could see why it was called the Crimson Volcano. Not only was glowing red molten lava spilling out of the top, but the entire volcano itself was red.

'Are we *sure* we have to look inside that thing?' Dylan called from his perch on Buttons. 'How do we know Glorious Old's bones are there? They weren't in that creepy cave that tried to eat us alive.'

'Which is exactly why we have to look in the volcano,' said Billy, urging Spark on even faster. 'As the bones weren't in the cave, they must be here. I have a gut feeling.'

'I hate it when you get that kind of feeling,' said Dylan.

Billy grinned over his shoulder at his friend, and then he saw something that made his blood run cold.

In the distance, the Dragons of Dawn were somehow gaining on them. Even though they didn't know what Billy and his friends were looking for, they wanted to destroy the human children and their dragons because they represented what the Dragons of Dawn hated most of all – peace between the two species.

'We don't have much time!' cried Ling-Fei, who had spotted the Dragons of Dawn at the same time as Billy. 'They're catching up to us!'

'We could always fight them off,' said Charlotte, brandishing a fist in the direction of the yellow and orange dragons. 'And then keep looking for the bones when we know they aren't on our tail.'

'There are too many of them,' said Spark. 'Even

with our powers combined, I do not know if we could take on that many dragons.'

'But we could at least slow them down,' said Xing. 'We do not all need to go into the volcano.'

'Xing's right,' said Billy.

'Of course I am,' said Xing. 'I am always right.'

'So we divide up?' said Jordan, warily watching the rapidly approaching pack of dragons. 'Some of us go into the volcano, and some of us try to stop the Dragons of Dawn?'

'What a choice,' said Dylan dryly. 'Death by volcano fire, or by dragon fire.'

'Nobody's dying,' said Billy with as much confidence as he could muster. 'And I'm the only one going into that volcano.'

'What are you talking about?' said Lola. 'Now is not the time to be the hero!'

'I'm the only one who can!' said Billy. They were nearly at the mouth of the volcano, and the smoke was making his eyes sting. 'I can use my agility power to scale down inside it and look for the bones. Xing and Ling-Fei can use their seeker magic to guide me, and the rest of you can distract the Dragons of Dawn.'

'I can help too!' squealed Midnight. 'I can use my power to hide the volcano while you're in there.'

'Great idea, Midnight,' said Jordan, beaming with pride at his dragon.

'Then it is settled,' Tank said in his low, rumbling voice. 'Billy will go into the volcano. Spark will keep watch from above, along with Midnight and Jordan, and Xing and Ling-Fei will guide Billy. The rest of us will try to slow down the Dragons of Dawn. We will not be able to beat them, but we can at least keep them from discovering what we are after.'

'I bet we can beat them,' said Lola with a ferocious grin. 'Come on, Neptune! Why don't we go and give them a big hello?' The huge sea dragon roared in approval and dived into the ocean, with Lola still hanging on tight.

'Neptune will be able to stun them momentarily with her sound blast, but the rest of us need to be ready to fight,' said Tank. 'Are you ready?'

'Always!' cried Charlotte. 'Come on!'

'Be careful in that volcano, Billy,' said Dylan anxiously before he and Buttons flew in the direction of the Dragons of Dawn.

'I'll be fine,' said Billy, but he felt his throat go dry as he gazed down into the molten core of the volcano. He sure hoped the bones they were looking for really were inside.

'There is something in there,' said Xing. 'I can feel it.'

'Me too,' said Ling-Fei.

Billy gulped. This was the best chance they had at finding the spirit of Glorious Old. The only chance. And without her help, all was lost.

The Claw

Even from high above the volcano, Billy could feel the heat pouring out of it. Beads of sweat dripped down his forehead.

'Billy, you all right, mate?' Jordan called out to him as they circled the top of the volcano.

Billy found he couldn't speak, but he managed a tight grin and gave Jordan a thumbs up.

Xing and Ling-Fei flew close to him and Spark. 'Something very powerful is definitely in there,' said Xing. 'Ling-Fei, do you feel it too?'

Ling-Fei nodded. 'Yes, but it's deep in the volcano. Billy, are you sure you can do this?'

Still unable to speak, Billy nodded. He could feel

his heart beating so fast he thought it might burst out of his chest, but he forced himself to stay as calm as possible. If he panicked, he'd never be able to survive going down inside the volcano.

'Your suit will help protect you, but you must be quick. And careful,' said Xing. 'You will be able to reach into the lava to grab the bones, but if you fall, the suit will not be able to withstand the heat of the lava for longer than a few seconds. You will be cooked. Do you understand?'

Again, all Billy could do was nod. His stomach was churning. He knew he was the only one who could do this, but he wished one of his friends could go with him, or at least his dragon. But Spark couldn't fit in the cavity of the volcano. She must have sensed him thinking about her, because she sent a wave of reassurance through their bond.

'I could try to freeze the lava using my ice power,' Spark offered out loud. 'But I do not know how the lava would react, or how long it would stay frozen.' She tilted her head as she studied the volcano. 'Perhaps if we had more time, I could test a section . . .'

Billy finally found his voice. 'We don't have time.

Let's just get this over with.' He glanced behind him and saw that Tank, Neptune and Buttons, with Charlotte, Lola and Dylan still on their backs, had almost reached the approaching Dragons of Dawn. 'Midnight, are you ready to cover us?'

'You got it!' cried Midnight. 'Those baddie dragons won't be able to see any of us when we're in my blackout bubble.'

'But you'll all be able to see me, right?' said Billy slightly nervously.

'Yep! Anyone inside the bubble will be able to see the others.' Midnight beamed. 'I've been practising!'

Billy grinned back at his dragon friend. Her optimism was contagious, and now he felt a little more confident that he could do the thing he'd just told everyone he could do.

'But be fast,' Midnight went on. 'I don't know how long I can hold the bubble for.' Then she took a deep breath, and Billy knew they had been blacked out.

Spark flew directly over the volcano opening. Smoke billowed out of it, so hot that Billy winced.

'Get in, grab the bones, get out,' he said. He glanced up at Spark. 'How will I know what to look for?'

'You will know when you find the bones. After all, you have seen dragon bones before,' said Spark. 'Now, are you ready?'

'Ready as I'll ever be to jump into a volcano while being pursued by angry dragons,' said Billy.

'I will never understand why humans use sarcasm as a coping mechanism,' sighed Xing. Then her eyes lit up as she moved nearer to the volcano. 'The bones are close. They are so steeped in ancient magic that they sing to me even from outside the volcano. Go now, Billy, and quickly.'

Before he could second guess himself, Billy flung himself off Spark's back and into the depths of the volcano. He thought he'd prepared for the heat, but when it hit him, it was like a punch in the face.

A steaming hot punch in the face.

His eyes immediately began to water and sweat poured down his forehead, getting into his eyes. And then he was in the volcano itself, and it somehow grew even hotter.

Using his agility power, he was able to land directly on the interior wall of the volcano. Luckily, his hands were protected by a buzzing electricity that he knew thrummed through his veins. It came from his affinity to the Lightning Pearl, and to Spark. This wasn't the first time that the electric shield had protected his hands and body. When they'd needed to find the Ember Flower to stop Charlotte from turning into stone, Ling-Fei had opened up the earth itself and Billy had scaled down inside it, much like he was doing now.

The memory bolstered him. He could do this.

But when he'd gone searching for the Ember Flower, there hadn't been as much lava, he thought as he quickly climbed out of the way of a wayward splash of molten magma. How was he supposed to find dragon bones in here?

Suddenly he heard Spark's voice in his head. *Billy, Xing says you must go deeper into the volcano.*

Billy looked up, and through the billowing smoke, he saw Xing and Spark flying around the opening of the volcano, watching his movements.

Easy for her to say, Billy thought back, but he carefully made his way deeper into the volcano, looking around for something, anything, that looked like a dragon bone.

I don't see anything, he thought to Spark, trying not to panic. *What if I can't find the bones?*

Xing says they must be in there because she can sense them. Keep looking.

'Dragon bones, dragon bones, where are you?' Billy hummed to himself as he clung to the interior of the volcano. He heard a roar outside the volcano, and then another closer one, and he realized with a sickening lurch that the Dragons of Dawn were nearby.

He hoped Midnight could keep up the blackout bubble even with an onslaught of dragons surrounding her. And he hoped that his friends were okay.

Billy. Spark's voice in his mind was sharp. *Stay focused.*

His vision was starting to go hazy. It was so hot down here. So hot. How could he find the dragon bones if he couldn't see clearly?

Spark's voice came again, more insistent. *Xing says you are nearly there. She says there is some sort of hollow near you where they must be.*

Billy felt along the wall of the volcano, his tongue stuck out in concentration, as he tried to find the hollow that Xing sensed. How could an entire dragon have ever fitted in here? It didn't make sense. And why had Billy been so sure they could trust a magical disappearing crane of all things . . .

His fingers snagged on something, and there was a clatter as a series of small rocks fell from the side of the volcano and down into the bubbling lava below. Something sharp had pricked his hand, so sharp it punctured the electric gloves he was wearing to scale the inside of the volcano. He hissed and pulled back, and then scrambled down lower, closer to the lava below. At least this way he could get a better look at what he assumed was the hollow Xing had been referring to.

And what he saw made his heart skip a beat.

It wasn't an entire dragon skeleton, but it was an unmistakable dragon claw. Smooth and curved, with a deadly sharp point, the claw was larger than Spark's claws, but smaller than Tank's.

Billy reached out and tugged on it, but it was stuck. He tugged harder.

Billy? Spark's panicked voice entered his head. *You have to get out of there. The volcano is rumbling.*

'I've almost got it!' he shouted out loud, as well as

down their bond. He was so focused on pulling out the claw that he wasn't thinking straight, or maybe it was the heat. He was feeling very dizzy now.

Billy pulled hard with one hand, the other hanging onto another crevice, while his feet remained planted against the interior wall of the volcano. Then he pulled as hard as he could, and suddenly something gave, almost as though he'd accidentally pulled a lever. Immediately, an unsettling feeling washed over him. It felt like a trap, as if Glorious Old had left the claw here on purpose to warn away intruders if they found it.

Then the claw came completely loose with a loud *pop*, and Billy nearly fell backwards. At least he had something now, but the rest of the dragon bones still had to be in there. He peered into the hollow, but it was empty. Billy's heart sank.

'I've got something!' he cried. 'But it's just the claw!'

'That will have to do!' Xing's voice echoed throughout the volcano. She was right at the top of it, yelling down at him. 'NOW GET OUT OF THERE, BILLY!'

'Coming!' Billy shouted back, and he began to

climb back up, carefully holding the dragon claw in one hand.

The volcano began to shake. Sweat poured down Billy's face and his eyes stung. There was so much smoke now that he couldn't see where to put his free hand, or even where to place his feet.

Suddenly, a roaring sound, not unlike a dragon roar, came from underneath Billy, and globs of lava started flying up past him. With a strange sense of detachment, he realized the volcano was about to erupt. With him inside it.

He climbed faster, as fast as he could, but the whole thing was shaking uncontrollably now and he couldn't see straight.

And then his finger slipped.

And Billy – who never lost his footing, whose agility power meant he could scramble up and down anything like a spider – fell.

17

A New Advantage

Billy clung to the claw as he fell. He tried to shout, but he was so shocked that the scream got trapped in his throat. It felt like a dream, but the heat rising up from the lava below him reminded him that this was indeed real life, and at that moment, he felt true fear course through his body.

As he fell through the volcano, the rumbling grew more and more intense, and Billy wondered in a delirious way if he would even reach the lava beneath him before the whole thing blew up.

Either way, he knew he was cooked. Literally. But he still had to try, so he twisted his body and reached for the wall of the volcano in the hope that he could grip onto it, or even use the claw as a kind of grappling hook.

But he couldn't.

Then, right when he was sure he was going to plunge into lava so hot that his suit wouldn't be able to withstand the heat, meaning he'd never see his family, friends or dragon again, a wide-eyed Jordan suddenly appeared in the air next to him.

Billy was so surprised he simply stared at Jordan in amazement.

Jordan stared back at him, clearly as amazed and confused as Billy was. 'Whoa,' he said, and then he grabbed Billy's arm. The next thing Billy knew, they were high in the sky, high above the volcano, staring down at it.

'Whoa,' Jordan said again, still holding onto Billy's arm, while Billy squeezed his hand tightly around the claw.

A split second later, they were on the edge of the outside of the volcano.

'JORDAN!' cried Midnight, diving down towards them. 'GET AWAY FROM THE VOLCANO!'

Billy blinked, and then he and Jordan were on

Midnight's back, and before he had time to blink again, they were suddenly in the sea.

'Whoa,' Jordan said a third time, clearly lost for words.

'DO THE THING!' Midnight yelled. 'QUICKLY! THE THING YOU JUST DID WITH BILLY! DO IT AND AIM FOR SPARK!'

Billy looked up and saw that Spark was in the distance, flying towards them.

'Er, okay,' said Jordan, and faster than Billy could comprehend, all three of them were suddenly in the air next to Spark.

'Billy,' said Spark, her voice full of emotion. 'You are safe.' She nudged his head with her own. 'I will be forever grateful to Jordan for rescuing you.' Then her eyes lit up. 'And you still have the claw. Come, ride with me.'

Billy was so stunned from everything that had just happened that his limbs felt wooden and limp, so Jordan helped move him onto Spark's back. Reeling, Billy settled himself onto his dragon, still clutching the claw he'd found in the volcano.

'Is he all right?' asked Jordan anxiously. 'He's

not said anything, and his eyes are like ... really, really wide.'

'I think he's in shock,' said Spark. 'But our bond means he will be able to stay astride me without even trying.' She bowed her head towards Jordan. 'I am so grateful you were able to save him. Even if I am not quite sure how you did it.'

'I don't even know how I did it myself!' said Jordan, rubbing his head in bewilderment.

'We can ponder that later,' said Xing, who was suddenly right next to them, Ling-Fei on her back. Billy realized they must have all flown away from the volcano when it began to rumble. And Jordan had been the only one who could save him. 'Right now we need to get away from that volcano.' No sooner had Xing finished her sentence, a huge boom rang out and the volcano erupted.

A massive plume of smoke exploded into the air, followed by a stream of lava that shot up and then out, until the entire outside of the Crimson Volcano was covered in molten hot red lava. As the lava hit the ocean, steam began to rise, and chunks of semi-hardened lava flew everywhere.

The blast had broken Midnight's blackout bubble and it sent Spark, Midnight and Xing careening through the sky, away from the explosion, but towards where Tank, Neptune, Buttons and their heart-bonded humans were still battling the Dragons of Dawn.

Billy's head rang as he tried to figure out what had just happened. One moment he'd been falling into the volcano, certain he was about to die, and the next Jordan had suddenly . . . *teleported* next to him. That was the only word for it. Teleported. And then he'd teleported them out of the volcano, onto Midnight, into the water, and somehow he'd even managed to teleport with Spark.

Even though his mind was spinning, Billy started to feel more like himself, and by the time they reached the battle between the Dragons of Dawn and his friends, he was almost completely back to normal. And he was glad of that, because he knew it was time for them to join the fight ahead.

There were twelve Dragons of Dawn, and currently only three dragons battling against them. Flame himself wasn't there, but it was still an uneven battle. If it was anyone but the dragons Billy knew, he'd have thought they wouldn't have stood a chance, but he knew their dragons were the fiercest dragons in any realm, and they wouldn't go down without a fight. And now they had backup.

Billy watched as one of the Dragons of Dawns sent a blast of flame right at Buttons, who narrowly dodged it. Neptune roared in protest, sending out her signature sound blast that momentarily froze the attacking dragon.

But it wasn't just Neptune. Billy watched in amazement as Lola swung her arms at another advancing Dragon of Dawn, and then all of the Dragons of Dawn seemed to be moving in slow motion – everything was except Lola and Neptune. Even a wave that was cresting had slowed down. Then Lola leaped off Neptune's neck and up onto Tank, and as soon as she made contact with him, Tank was suddenly able to move quickly too, sending a fire blast at one of the Dragons of Dawn and knocking the other out of the sky with his tail. The Dragons of Dawn were moving so slowly, like bees stuck in honey, making it easy for Tank to defeat them.

Was Lola *controlling time*? It reminded Billy of what

she'd done when they'd gone to rescue Neptune from TURBO at the White Cliffs of Dover.

Then the spell was broken and four Dragons of Dawn charged at Tank all at once. That snapped Billy out of his thoughts. He had to focus, and he had to make sure he kept hold of the claw. He was still clutching it in his hand, so tightly that it made his fingers ache.

'Spark,' he said, his voice hoarse from inhaling so much smoke while in the volcano. 'Are we winning?' He still couldn't think straight.

'We will be,' said Spark. 'Especially now that Lola's and Jordan's powers have awoken. Look!'

Billy began watching Jordan, and was certain he really was teleporting. It was as if Jordan and Midnight were blinking in and out of existence. One moment they were next to Billy and Spark, the next they were right in front of a Dragon of Dawn, distracting it enough for Buttons to send out a blast of green fire. Midnight was laughing with glee and Jordan had a look of fierce concentration on his face.

'But they don't have pearls,' said Billy, trying to understand how this was all happening.

The Eight Great Treasures, the pearls that he and his friends had been given by their dragons, had awoken their own inherent powers. A dragon bond was needed first, but if a human with a dragon bond had a pearl, they'd also gain a power. Billy's was agility, Dylan's was charm and persuasion, Charlotte's was super strength and Ling-Fei's was control over nature and an ability to sense living things.

'Something else must have awoken their powers,' said Spark. 'But in this moment, I am grateful for them. Jordan saved your life, and now it looks as if his and Lola's powers are giving us the advantage over the Dragons of Dawn.'

'Come on,' said Billy, urging Spark forward. 'Let's go help them win!'

'I am worried about you,' said Spark. 'That is why I am staying back for now. You nearly died in that volcano. I felt it down our bond.'

Billy swallowed, his mouth suddenly dry at hearing Spark speak so bluntly about how close he'd been to death.

'I was about to fly in myself when I saw Jordan

disappear off Midnight's back, and then, a moment later, he was back up in the air, gripping you by the arm. He is a true friend. I am very glad he has joined us.'

'Me too,' said Billy, watching as his friend blinked in and out of the air, distracting and attacking the Dragons of Dawn. 'And I'm fine now, really. Buttons can take a look at me later.'

'If you are sure,' said Spark, sounding uncertain.

'I am,' said Billy. 'I can't let my friends fight without me. Come on!'

With a roar, Spark plunged into the fray, sending out blasts of electricity at any Dragon of Dawn in her path.

Billy suddenly felt a buzzing in his hand. He glanced down in surprise at the claw he had taken from the volcano. It was glowing and vibrating with power. He held it aloft in shock.

A Dragon of Dawn, one of a similar size to Spark with spikes all the way down its back, who had been advancing towards them menacingly, stopped in mid-air as it stared at the claw.

'Is that the claw of Glorious Old?' it shouted.

Billy became instantly wary. What if this dragon tried to take the claw from him? Or told Flame what they'd found?

'I can tell that it is, so do not deny it,' the spiked dragon went on. 'I know that it came from the Crimson Volcano, but what I do not know is what you are doing with it.'

Billy couldn't hold back any longer. 'We're trying to help! We want to help the dragons, despite what Flame says.'

The spiked dragon flew a little closer. Billy felt Spark tense. *Wait and see what this dragon has to say*, Billy thought down their bond.

And then, to Billy's surprise, the dragon's scales slowly began to change colour from yellow and orange, the colours that signified it was a Dragon of Dawn, to pale green with gold flecks.

'You say you want to help? I thought all humans hated dragons. I have never met one before, you know,' said the pale green dragon.

'I could never hate dragons,' said Billy vehemently. 'I love my dragon. We all do. We're heart-bonded with them and want to help as many as we can.'

'But I heard Flame was put in chains,' said the pale green dragon. 'How do you explain that?'

'Some humans want to use dragon power for their own advantage,' Billy admitted. 'But that's because they don't understand dragons. We want to change that.'

'I do not know if that is possible,' said the green dragon. 'Look around. Dragons are battling dragons. That is not a sign of peace.'

'We know,' said Billy sadly, watching as the battle raged on around them. 'That's why we want to find Glorious Old. We need to summon her to help us find a safe home for dragons.'

The pale green dragon was almost completely green now, the signs of its allegiance to the Dragons of Dawn having disappeared. 'You will not find her here,' the dragon went on, seemingly unaware of its scales changing before everyone. 'You may have found her claw, but she did not spend her last moments in the Crimson Volcano.'

Billy held his breath, waiting for the dragon to keep speaking. It paused and then glanced at its own claws as it realized it had changed back to green. 'I feel different,' it murmured, almost to itself. 'Like my mind was hazy and now it is clear.' It looked around at the battling dragons. 'I did not want to fight you, but something in my head told me I had to. Is that not peculiar?'

Billy was certain Flame was doing something to convince dragons to join him, something that sounded a lot like hypnosis.

'I'm glad you're feeling like yourself again,' he said to the green dragon. 'Now can you tell me more about Glorious Old? Do you know where her bones are?'

'Oh, yes,' said the dragon. 'Glorious Old is my ancestor. My family has always known where her bones are. But even if you know, it will not help you.'

'What do you mean?' asked Billy.

'Her final resting place is the Dark Desert. She chose to die there so her bones would never be found.'

Remember Who You Are

'No,' whispered Spark. 'It cannot be.'

'It is,' said the pale green dragon. 'I do not lie. I have no reason to lie to you. I know my dragon brethren are battling you, but I have lost that urge.' The dragon inspected its own claws again. 'It is very curious that my scales have changed.' It glanced back up at Billy and Spark. 'I will leave you now. I have questions for Flame, the dragon who convinced me to change my scales. I must find it back in London.'

'Is Flame still in London?' asked Billy.

'Yes, it continues to ask other dragons to join the Dragons of Dawn, convincing them ... somehow.' The green dragon gazed at Billy. 'He has made

London his home, and he will not leave it willingly, even if you do find a new place for dragons.'

'We have to try,' said Billy stubbornly.

'I wish you luck,' said the green dragon. It gazed around at the battle still happening around them. 'And some advice – try to remind these dragons who they were before they became Dragons of Dawn. Seeing Glorious Old's claw reminded me who I am.'

Then the pale green dragon flew off before Billy could ask it any more questions.

'If you're done having a chit-chat with that dragon, we could use some help!' yelled Charlotte from where she and Tank were battling three Dragons of Dawn at once.

'Xing,' cried Spark. 'On my signal, put up a wall of reflection!'

'I do not know what you are planning,' said Xing.

'Just do it!' pleaded Spark. 'DRAGONS!' she roared, louder than Billy had ever heard her. 'REMEMBER WHO YOU ARE!'

Spark shot down her ice power so the thrashing sea stilled and became shining ice. With a knowing nod, Xing blasted the frozen sea with her own power, creating an enchantment so the ice reflected their images back to them.

The Dragons of Dawn all stared down in confusion at their reflections.

'Who is that?' said one with four tails. 'Is that me? My scales should be purple!'

'Flame, your leader, has changed your hearts and your scales,' said Spark. 'If you battle us of your own free will, then we will continue. But we have no interest in fighting any dragon that is under another dragon's persuasion.'

Right before their eyes, five of the dragons began to change colour, including the one with four tails. But the other six stayed yellow and orange.

'I hate humans,' one of them hissed, baring its teeth. It had five spikes covering its head, almost creating the shape of a star. 'I welcomed Flame's message about dragons bonding together. We do not need humans. We never did and we never will. It was a mistake to begin to bond with them.'

'I never wanted to battle anyone,' said the four-tailed purple dragon. 'But Flame told me humans would force me to fight for their own entertainment every day. It said you were the ones we needed to destroy to keep that from happening.'

'I would *never* let dragons be used for that!' said Charlotte.

'Me neither!' added Lola.

'We respect dragons,' said Ling-Fei.

'We're on your side,' said Billy. 'Or . . . we're on the side of dragons who want peace.'

'Flame tricked me,' muttered the four-tailed purple dragon.

'Flame is trying to protect you from humans!' said the star-headed dragon.

'But these humans are children,' said the four-tailed dragon. 'And children have the purest hearts of all humans. All dragons know this.'

As it spoke, the star-headed dragon's yellow scales darkened to a deep blue, until it was clear that it was no longer aligned with the Dragons of Dawn. The now blue star-headed dragon glared at Billy and the other humans. 'Just because I am not going to fry you, does not mean I like you. Be gone before I change my mind.'

'Bold of you to suggest you could fry us when

we have been beating you in this battle,' said Tank. 'And now that there are fewer of you, we could end it here and now.'

'We could have ended it at any moment,' growled Neptune. 'The only reason the battle is still going on is because we did not want to kill you. As you say, the human children have pure hearts. They do not kill if they can help it. But I am more vengeful.' Neptune glared at the remaining Dragons of Dawn. 'I would disappear if I were you. Before we make you.'

'We will meet again,' said one of the dragons who was still brandishing the orange and yellow Dragon of Dawn scales. 'And when we do, there will be more of us.'

'Perhaps then you will actually be a challenge,' said Xing. 'Now, do as we say and be gone.'

'And be glad we reminded you who you are,' said Spark. 'Remember, not every dragon can be trusted.'

With a final glare, the last Dragons of Dawn flew off together and the others scattered, leaving the kids and their dragons alone, hovering over the sea.

*

'What the heck happened in that volcano?' said Charlotte.

'And is that Glorious Old's claw? Can we summon her now?' asked Lola.

'Yes, it's the claw, but, no, we can't summon her. And I have a question for you,' said Billy. 'Can you control time?'

Lola laughed and her cheeks flushed. 'I . . . I'm not really sure. I can definitely do something.'

'She slows time for a short period,' said Neptune. 'It is similar to how I can freeze creatures with my sound blast. They are linked, somehow.'

'And you,' Billy looked at Jordan. 'You can teleport?'

Jordan shrugged. 'Apparently. I saw you about to fall into the lava, and I wanted to catch you, then suddenly I was there. And we were out of the volcano a second later. The more I did it, the better I could focus my power.'

'You guys definitely got the coolest powers,' said Dylan.

'Hey! I resent that,' said Charlotte. 'And how did you two even get powers without pearls?'

'We have much to discuss,' said Spark. 'But not much time. We must go to the Dark Desert.'

'The Dark Desert? It is impossible,' said Xing. 'The Dark Desert is as dark as the inside of a black hole. No light, not even dragon-created light, can shine there.'

Midnight let out a distressed squeak. 'I like the dark, but I don't want to go somewhere that swallows light.'

'It is where Glorious Old's bones are,' said Spark. 'We must try.'

'But we have the claw!' said Jordan.

'It's not enough,' said Buttons. 'We need her bones.'

'Glorious Old left her claw in the volcano on purpose,' said Billy. 'It was some sort of trap. When I pulled it free, the volcano erupted. She knew someone would find it, and she wanted to warn them away.'

'Well, maybe we should listen to her warning,' said Dylan with a nervous laugh.

'If her claw can be found, so can the rest of her,' said Spark. 'There must be a way.'

'What if the Dark Desert has fallen into the Human Realm?' said Midnight. 'Like the Crimson Volcano?'

Xing closed her eyes. 'It has not,' she said after a long moment. 'I cannot sense it anywhere in this realm. We must go back to the Dragon Realm and into the Dark Desert.'

This time, Xing created the portal. She had the best sense of where they needed to go in the Dragon Realm.

'I will take us as close as we can go, but we cannot portal directly into the Dark Desert,' she said.

'So it's just going to be . . . dark?' said Lola. 'I don't understand how we're meant to find anything if we can't see.'

'Or how we're meant to, you know, stay alive, somewhere where anything could sneak up and attack us,' said Dylan.

'I'm with Dylan on this one,' said Jordan.

'I'll protect you!' said Midnight. 'In light or dark, I'll be there.'

'Midnight is right. Our bond is stronger than any darkness,' said Tank. 'We will act as the light for each other.'

'Can I get that motivational saying on a T-shirt?' said Dylan.

'Dylan!' chided Ling-Fei. 'I think it's nice, and it's true!'

'Are you ... mocking me?' said Tank, his voice dangerously low.

'Yeah, Dylan, are you mocking Tank?' said Charlotte with a wicked grin.

'No! Of course not. Well, maybe just a tiny bit. Come on! Our bond is stronger than any darkness? Even for a dragon that's a little bit extra.'

'What is extra?' said Tank. 'Extra what?'

'Never mind. I agree with you. Let's go into the darkness with our bond that is like a candle that cannot be extinguished or whatever you said,' said Dylan.

'Oh! I like that,' said Buttons approvingly. 'A bond that cannot be extinguished!'

'There are a lot of metaphors to have fun with,' said Dylan. 'I'm just getting started.'

'I sense you are still joking,' said Tank. 'I find humans so baffling. How can one joke at such a serious time?'

'Serious times are the best times for joking,' said Jordan. 'The only way to get through the hard bits is with banter.'

'Jordan's right,' said Billy, grinning at his friends. 'If

I didn't have you guys by my side, everything would be way worse.'

'If you didn't have us by your side, you'd probably be dead,' said Charlotte.

'Yeah, come on, Billy. I'm good for more than just jokes,' said Dylan, grinning back at him.

'All right, all right,' said Billy. 'I couldn't do any of this without you all.'

'Your strength has always come from your bond as friends,' said Spark. 'And it is true that you children make the hard bits, as you call them, much better.' She turned to Xing. 'Is the portal ready?'

Xing flicked her tail in the direction of a swirling pool in the sea below. 'It is.'

'We will follow you,' said Spark.

'To the Dragon Realm, and to the Dark Desert!' said Billy, and he held the claw aloft, hoping it would guide them to Glorious Old's bones.

The Dark Desert

When they exited the portal, Billy didn't recognize where they were. It was a part of the Dragon Realm he'd never been to before.

The air was hazy, the ground was cracked and dry and there was nothing to see for miles. Except for a giant black cloud in front of them. It was so big that it started at ground level and stretched up high into the sky. It was the darkest black Billy had ever seen, darker than when he closed his eyes tight or when he looked up at the night sky. The edges were blurry, and it almost looked as if someone had taken a black marker and scrawled a circle against the sky. When the wind blew, the cloud shook but stayed grounded.

Billy was still clutching the dragon claw, and he gripped it a little tighter as he gazed at the black cloud.

'We have to go inside that thing, don't we?' said Dylan with a groan.

'That is indeed where the Dark Desert lies,' said Buttons. 'It's not a place most dragons venture.'

'Surely Tank can light the way with his flame, or Spark with her electricity, right?' said Charlotte. 'There has to be some way for us to be able to see in there.'

'My horns always glow,' added Midnight.

'No, the Dark Desert extinguishes all light, even your horns, Midnight. And I do not know what, or whom, we will find when we enter,' said Spark.

'Well, hopefully we'll find the bones,' said Jordan. 'Since that's what we came here for.'

'Why is so little known about the Dark Desert?' said Billy, eyeing the big black cloud warily.

'Because few who enter it ever come out.' Xing paused to let her words sink in, and Billy felt a shiver of goosebumps rise up on his skin at the warning. 'And those who do survive cannot say what they have seen due to the darkness,' said Xing.

'Well, as encouraging as that little fact is,' said Lola, 'we might as well go in now and get it over with.'

Billy smiled at her, appreciating her no-nonsense can-do attitude. It felt as if she and Jordan had always been part of their crew. He couldn't imagine doing this without them now.

'I am not meant for the desert,' grumbled Neptune. 'I belong in the sea. But I go where Lola goes, where you all go.'

'Neptune, that's so sweet,' said Ling-Fei, beaming up at the giant dragon. She glanced at Xing. 'You could learn to be a little more like that.'

Xing snorted. 'I let my actions speak louder than my words. But if you must hear it out loud, of course I go where you go.'

Ling-Fei stroked Xing between her antlers. 'I'm very glad you're my dragon,' she said.

'And *I'm* very glad you're coming in there with us. We need your seeker powers now more than ever,' said Billy. 'Do we have a plan for finding the bones? Or are we just going to wander around in the dark until we stumble on them?'

'The dark in a literal sense,' added Dylan. 'Not

just a metaphorical one. Although I suppose it's also metaphorical . . .'

'Not helpful, Dylan,' said Charlotte.

'The plan is that we all go in together and hope Xing can sense where the bones are in the same way she knew where the desert itself would be located,' said Ling-Fei. 'Xing will be able to do it, I'm sure of it.'

'And I guess we just cross our fingers that the Dark Desert doesn't fall into the Human Realm while we're inside it?' said Lola.

'It will eventually. If not today, perhaps tomorrow. Or the day after. But soon there will be nothing left of the Dragon Realm, and the Human Realm will be for ever altered,' said Tank.

'Summoning Glorious Old and locating the Hidden Realm is the only option left to help us find a safe place for dragons who don't want to live alongside humans,' said Buttons. 'It's a shame as I'd hoped peace would be possible.'

'The way humans and dragons have been acting towards each other makes me think almost all dragons will be better off living separately in the Hidden Realm,' said Lola.

Billy eyed the giant black cloud in front of them. Every instinct told him to run away from it because something terrible was waiting inside. He knew how important it was to trust his instincts, but this was the only way to bring some semblance of peace to the world.

He squared his shoulders and looked at his friends and their dragons.

'We can do this,' he said. 'We go in ready to fight. We stick together. We find the bones.'

'Well, when you put it that way, it sounds practically easy,' said Dylan.

'We should go on foot,' Billy added. 'The bones will be on the ground, and if we're in the air, we'll never find them.'

'We should probably still sit on our dragons if they're going on foot,' said Charlotte. 'I don't want Tank to accidentally step on me.'

'I would never,' said Tank, clearly affronted.

'You might if you can't see me,' said Charlotte. She scrambled up on his head. 'I feel safest up here anyway.'

'Some of us do not walk,' sniffed Xing. 'But I will

fly low to the ground and lead the way, since I am the one who will be able to sense the bones.'

'There will be creatures in the Dark Desert that will be used to not being able to see,' said Spark. 'Creatures that might be hungry. You must stay alert.'

'Well, I for one have no intention of becoming a snack,' said Jordan.

'Me neither!' said Midnight. 'And I bet my horns will still glow in there. Darkness is a friend of mine, after all.'

'There's only one way to find out,' said Billy. 'Let's go.'

As they drew up next to the edge of the black cloud that contained the Dark Desert, Billy paused. He reached his hand out and it easily passed into the darkness and out of view, as if he didn't have a hand at all. The darkness had swallowed it completely.

Billy gulped.

And then something occurred to him. 'We're going to lose each other in there,' he said. 'We have to hold hands . . . or tails.'

'I do not like the idea of having you all hang

onto my tail,' grumbled Xing. 'But I suppose it is a good idea.'

They positioned themselves into a line. Xing and Ling-Fei went first, with Midnight holding her tail and Jordan on her back. Buttons and Dylan came next, then Spark and Billy, Tank and Charlotte and last was Neptune and Lola.

'In we go,' said Xing, and she disappeared into the darkness.

Midnight followed, and Billy heard her yelp as she entered the desert. He stared very hard at Buttons's tail in front of him, but as soon as he'd passed through the black cloud, the darkness was absolute.

Billy blinked instinctively, his eyes straining in the dark to try to see something ... anything.

He heard Dylan's voice sound out ahead of him. 'Wow, at least now we know some of the stories are true. This place is, like, seriously dark.'

'Even my horns aren't glowing,' said Midnight, sounding disappointed.

'Quiet,' snapped Xing from further up the chain, 'I need to focus. I can sense ... something.'

'Hopefully it's the bones?' said Billy.

'There are living things in here,' whispered Ling-Fei.

'Yes, I can hear their heartbeats,' said Spark quietly.

A chill went up Billy's spine. He knew, of course, that there would be living creatures in the Dark Desert, but he'd hoped they wouldn't come across any of them.

'Is everyone in here?' he said, glancing over his shoulder, even though he couldn't see anything. 'Lola? Neptune?'

'I'm here!' Lola called back.

'We should not be so loud,' hissed Xing. 'The creatures in here will have hearing far superior even to ours . . .'

She suddenly went quiet, and then a commotion started at the front of the chain.

'Xing! Why'd you stop?' cried Jordan. 'Midnight just tripped on your tail!'

'And knocked me over,' grumbled Buttons.

'There is something here,' Xing hissed back. 'We need to stay still! I can hear it approaching.'

Billy blinked in the darkness, because suddenly it wasn't quite as dark. He could see a shape, moving and bobbing around. A glowing shape that reminded him of the crane. Neon rainbow colours in the shape of a person. A person floating in the air. No, a person riding a dragon, right in front of him. Three people. Jordan, Dylan and Ling-Fei. They were all glowing, not completely, but patches on them were glowing.

He raised his own hand and flecks of neon blue and pink shone in the dark. He was glowing too. 'You guys! We're glowing! There's something all over us and it's glowing!'

But only the children were glowing, not the dragons. And when Billy looked behind him, he saw that Lola shone much more brightly than Charlotte, who only had a few flecks of glimmering colour on her.

The glow allowed Billy to see a little bit of his surroundings. He could see parts of the dragons, he could see the shape of what looked like distant sand dunes, and he could see . . .

'WATCH OUT!' cried Charlotte, as a nightmarish creature leaped at Billy with so much force that it knocked him off Spark's back and into the sand.

Fanged Tiger-Rats

Billy tumbled to the ground, almost dropping the dragon claw, as the creature pinned him to the sand. He was only able to see it from the glow coming from his own body, but what he saw made his stomach clench with terror.

The bottom half of the creature's face was all mouth, and when it unhinged its enormous jaw, huge fangs protruded out. Above its mouth were wide, flat nostrils, almost like a snake. And where its eyes should have been were empty holes. Triangular ears pointed back from its head and its body resembled that of a giant rodent, a long scaly tail whipping behind it.

It looked like a rat crossed with a sabre-toothed tiger, with a little bit of snake added to the mix. And it was salivating all over Billy. Its breath was terrible, and as its sharp claws pressed against him, Billy knew that without his super-suit, his skin would have been ripped to shreds.

He tried to scramble out from under the creature but it was too strong.

'Spark!' Billy yelled, both aloud and down their bond, and then right as the creature was about to sink its fangs into his neck, Spark was there, blasting it with her power.

Spark's power gave off no light, and invisible electricity crackled as it struck the fanged rat. The creature screamed and Billy smelled burned hair as Spark fried it.

Billy pushed the dead thing off him and staggered to his feet. 'What was that?' he choked out between ragged breaths.

'A fanged tiger-rat!' cried Midnight. 'I thought they were made up to scare hatchlings! I didn't know they were real!'

'Oh, they're real all right, and it looks as if there's

more of them coming!' said Dylan, pointing out into the darkness.

Billy could only see as far as the glow allowed him to, but he could make out the shapes of the creatures as they approached, and he could hear their panting and the sound of their clawed paws on the sand as they raced towards the group.

'We can take on giant rodents,' he said. 'Come on!'

But as the battle began, he realized that the fanged tiger-rats weren't to be underestimated. They were fast, and they clearly didn't need to be able to see.

One jumped on Tank's leg and sank its fangs into it. Tank roared in pain and kicked it off, and Billy watched as it soared through the air, landed in a heap on the sand and then immediately hopped back up and attacked the next nearest dragon.

'Neptune! Can you use your sound blast to freeze them?' cried Billy.

'I cannot aim well enough in the dark – I might take out one of our own!' Neptune called back.

'I'll do a slow-time snap!' said Lola. 'But get ready for it!'

Even though Billy had seen and experienced it

before, having Lola slow down time still came as a shock. He tried to lift his arm, but it felt incredibly heavy and moved so slowly. But Lola appeared to be moving at hyper-speed, and when she touched him, he felt as though he'd been zapped awake. Suddenly, he could move at his normal speed again, and he watched as Lola did the same to his friends.

He kicked out at a slow-moving fanged tiger-rat, sending it flying into a nearby sand dune where it lay stunned.

'Try not to hurt them!' cried Ling-Fei. 'We've come into their land. It isn't their fault they see us as food!'

'They don't see us at all!' yelled back Charlotte. 'And I'm sorry, but we need to protect ourselves!' She picked one up and swung it over her head, throwing it into the distance. 'I refuse to let a giant rodent be the death of me.'

'We would never let that happen,' said Tank as he blasted one with invisible flames.

The dragons were clearly more powerful, but the fanged tiger-rats had the element of surprise and numbers on their side. Billy and the others could only see the fanged tiger-rats when they were close enough to be lit up by the strange glow coming off the children. And by that time, the fanged tiger-rats already had the advantage. It seemed as if no sooner than they'd dealt with one, another came flying out of the sand.

And then Billy saw something in the shadows that made him stop in his tracks.

One of the fanged tiger-rats was dragging a large bone under a dune.

A dragon bone.

'THEY HAVE THE BONES!' he cried.

'Midnight! What else do you know about fanged tiger-rats?' yelled Jordan as he teleported out of the way of one running at him.

'They use their hearing and smell to track their prey!' Midnight called back as she swung her horns towards one, throwing it in front of Spark, who shocked it with her electric power.

Billy thought quickly. 'Neptune! Use a sound blast to confuse them! Shoot it over there, away from the dunes, and hopefully they'll follow the sound!'

'Good thinking, Billy!' said Lola.

'I will try it,' said Neptune. 'But you must all

stay very still so the creatures are not distracted by any sound you make.' Then Neptune turned away from the group and from the dune where Billy had spied the bone, and shot her sound blast into the distance.

The fanged tiger-rats froze, and then lifted their heads at the sound. Billy was sure his heart was hammering so loudly that they'd be able to hear it, but they stayed focused on Neptune's sound blast.

'We have to hope they follow their hearing and don't realize there's nothing over there because of the lack of smell,' whispered Buttons.

'I can do an enchantment to add a smell,' said Xing. 'Ling-Fei, you stay here with Spark.'

She dropped Xing onto Spark's back and zoomed off in the direction in which Neptune had sent the sound blast. Moments later, she'd returned, and whatever she'd done must have worked, because the fanged tiger-rats turned and disappeared into the dark.

'We do not have much time,' said Xing. 'The enchantment will only last so long. The creatures will soon figure out that there is nothing there and they will come back. There may even be more of them.'

'Or another creature that lives in the dark could find us,' said Tank.

'We don't need much time,' said Billy, racing to the dune where he'd seen the fanged tiger-rat drag the bone. He held his glowing hand out to guide him like a torch. 'I think we've found the bones.'

Glorious Old

Billy carefully put the claw in his pocket so he could dig through the sand dune. And there it was – a pile of dragon bones. There weren't even teeth marks on the bones from the fanged tiger-rats gnawing at them. Billy remembered that only dragon claws or teeth could mark a dragon bone.

'There are so many bones!' said Jordan. 'How are we going to put them together to summon Glorious Old's spirit, especially when we can't see anything?'

'Look!' gasped Ling-Fei. 'The bones! They're glowing like we are!'

'But only the bones that we touch,' said Lola,

turning one over and inspecting it. The one she held glowed pale yellow and the next one a bright blue.

Now that they weren't battling the fanged tiger-rats, Billy was able to observe his friends more closely. It looked as if they were all splattered in some sort of glow-in-the-dark paint, which didn't make any sense. Unless . . .

'The glowing crane! And that goop in the cave! It must be what's making us glow! We were always meant to come here! It's all connected!'

Billy felt chills rise up the back of his neck as he realized that they were exactly where they were supposed to be. If they hadn't gone to the Cave of Secrets first, they not only wouldn't have been able to see the bones or each other, they most likely would have fallen prey to the fanged tiger-rats.

He reached back into his pocket for the claw and, sure enough, when his fingers gripped it, the claw started to glow as well.

Charlotte began to laugh as she inspected her arms, which were less flecked with the bioluminescent goop than everyone else's. 'Some of it must have washed off when I went in the Forgotten Sea!' she said. 'I was wondering why I wasn't glowing as much as the rest of you.'

As they began to lay the bones out on the sand and connect them, the bones glowed even brighter, each one a different colour. The dragons helped them with the placement.

'No, no, that one goes here, not there,' said Xing.

'And I think this one goes here,' said Buttons, pointing to the other side of the skeleton's ribcage.

At last, they were ready to place the final piece – the dragon skull. Everyone went quiet for a moment. Billy bowed his head respectfully, and together with his friends, they carefully dusted off the sand from the skull and placed it at the top of the skeleton. Billy held his breath, waiting for something to happen.

But nothing did. The dragon skeleton remained that . . . a skeleton in the sand.

'That was anticlimactic,' said Dylan.

'Something's missing,' said Ling-Fei, staring intently at the skeleton.

'Billy! The claw! The one you found in the volcano,' said Jordan. 'Maybe that's what's missing?'

'Of course,' said Billy, reaching into his pocket. 'This must be the last piece.'

'I sure hope it is, otherwise we're out of luck,' said Charlotte.

'It has to be,' said Billy, because suddenly he felt certain of it, as if the strands of destiny were coming together as he knelt in the sand and placed the claw next to the dragon's knuckle bone.

The entire skeleton suddenly began to shimmer.

'Get back,' said Spark. 'We do not know what is going to happen.'

The glowing skeleton shimmered and shone, sending a kaleidoscope of colour up into the darkness. It looked like an invisible hand was painting the Dark Desert sky. Billy stared open-mouthed in wonder at the spectacle overhead. More and more colours rose out of the skeleton, sending splashes of blue and purple and green across the desert.

And then, in the middle of all of the splashes of colour, an eye appeared, staring down at them.

Billy was so shocked that he nearly fell over into the skeleton itself.

The eye was large, and it blinked as it stared down

at the humans and dragons gathered in the desert. Another eye appeared next, followed by a set of teeth.

'It is her,' Xing whispered reverently, before bowing her head. 'It is Glorious Old. We have found her.'

All the dragons bowed their heads, but Billy couldn't tear his eyes away from the sight of a dragon appearing piece by piece in the night sky. The colours that rose out of the skeleton coalesced together to create rainbow-coloured clouds. They moved quickly, taking shape against the black sky, forming a dragon made of clouds.

The next thing to appear was a long thin snout, almost like a crocodile, the mouth opening and the teeth glinting. Her eyes opened again, and this time they were sitting on top of her head, gazing down at them. Then the clouds formed two spiralling horns behind her eyes, and a wispy mane that fanned out around her head, almost like a lion. From behind her head, the clouds stretched out, forming a long and slender body, like a powerful serpent. It thinned into a long tail, and then with a burst of colour, huge cloud wings exploded out of her sides. Smaller wisps of cloud formed her arms and legs, but by far her most prominent features were the giant wings, her long snout, spiralling horns and, of course, her eyes.

Eyes that were glaring down at them.

'Who dares disturb me?' she roared. Her voice sounded ancient and it echoed all around them.

Billy glanced at the dragons and he saw an expression on their faces that he'd never seen before. They looked afraid.

'We do not mean to disturb your rest,' said Spark, still keeping her head down.

'You certainly did not form my skeleton for the fun of it,' Glorious Old said. 'I made sure it was very difficult to do, and yet you have achieved it. Let me take a closer look at you.' She squinted down at them and her eyes narrowed in anger. 'HUMANS! YOU DARE BRING HUMANS TO MY BONES!'

She dived down towards them, flying so fast that the clouds scattered. Her glare was trained on Billy and he tensed, waiting for her strike, but she flew *through* him. A moment later, she had reassembled herself out of sand, in the same shape she had been in cloud form, her eyes and teeth unchanged.

'It is infuriating that I cannot touch you,' she said with another glare.

And Billy suddenly realized that of course she wouldn't be able to touch them – she was a spirit after all, having been slain by a human. Overcome with awe, and sadness that a human killed such a magnificent dragon, he fell to his knees. 'Glorious Old, we're not like the human who slayed you.'

She flew close to him again, but slowly this time. The sand fell away and she took her cloud form once more. 'Oh, are you not? Is it because you are a young human? A child? Your heart may be pure now, but one day you too will be the kind of human who can slay a dragon.'

'Glorious Old, these children are all heart-bonded to dragons. To us,' said Tank. 'They would never slay a dragon.'

'I once thought that humans could never, would never, slay a dragon. The idea was laughable. But look at me now. I am stuck here for ever, tethered for reasons I do not know. My spirit longs to be a star, longs to be free. A human killed me before I achieved my destiny, and now I must remain here.'

Charlotte cleared her throat. 'With all due respect, Glorious Old, ma'am, wouldn't you have a better chance of achieving your destiny if you weren't hiding here in the Dark Desert?'

Glorious Old looked Charlotte up and down. 'Well, you are bold. Do you not think that I spent centuries roaming the realm? Can you even comprehend so much time? My spirit has been *everywhere*, trying to find what my destiny might have been. I now believe I am destined to be tethered to this realm for ever.'

'You know, that might change sooner than you think,' said Dylan. 'This realm isn't going to exist much longer.'

Glorious Old stilled. 'What do you mean, child?'

'It's why we've come to find you!' Billy burst out.

'I did not want to be found,' said Glorious Old, looking away. 'It is why the Dark Desert is my final resting place – so that no dragon and certainly no human would be able to find me.' She turned her gaze on Billy. 'And yet, you have.'

'We need your help,' said Billy.

'Humans always need something from me. They

take, take, take,' said Glorious Old. 'I will never help another human again.'

'But we've worked so hard to find you!' said Lola. 'And you're right, you didn't make it easy!'

'Yeah, there were so many steps!' said Jordan. 'First, we went to your cave, which was a mission in itself, and then we met this neon crane. I still don't know if it was trying to help us or not.'

'My crane! She is still there? My dearest, most loyal companion,' said Glorious Old. 'I knew you went to my cave. It is why you are all glowing. But I will admit, I am surprised that my crane did not lead you deeper into the cave to become a snack. The cave likes to feed on living things, you know.'

'Oh, we know,' said Dylan.

'The honourable crane helped us in the end,' said Ling-Fei. 'Just as I believe you will help us, Glorious Old.' She bowed her head.

Glorious Old blinked at Ling-Fei. 'Your heart is especially good. It practically shines out of you.'

'That is my human,' said Xing proudly.

'I can read all of your hearts,' grumbled Glorious Old. 'It is my curse, being the first and oldest dragon.'

'Then you know we're good!' said Charlotte. 'So you'll help us?'

'I know you are good now. But I also know hearts can change. I trusted a human once, and he used my own sword against me.' Glorious Old turned away.

'Your heart-bonded human slayed you?' Billy felt sick at the very thought.

'No, we were not heart-bonded, but it was a human whom I trusted. They betrayed me, as all humans do to dragons eventually.' Glorious Old closed her eyes, and her cloud body began to fade away.

'We went to your volcano too,' said Jordan quickly. 'Billy dived down into it looking for your bones.'

An eye quickly flashed open in the dark, but just the one. 'I did notice you had found my claw. That was clever. Very few ever make it into the Dark Desert, and none have come with the claw. I will admit that is impressive.'

'You're our last hope, Glorious Old,' Billy said, his voice shaking with emotion. He desperately hoped she'd agree to help them.

Glorious Old opened her other eye. 'Oh, "Glorious

Old" makes me sound ... well, it makes me sound so old!'

'Er, aren't you the oldest dragon, like ever?' said Dylan.

'Yes, but I do not like being reminded of it every moment of every day.' The clouds reappeared, forming her body again. Her teeth glinted as she gave them a crescent moon smile. 'If I am going to have to talk to you, please, call me Glory.'

A Dragon In Any Form

'So,' said Glory. 'What do you need from me?'

Billy knew they needed to be honest. 'We want you to show us the Hidden Realm.'

Glory began to laugh, tossing her head back and chuckling with her cloud mouth wide open. 'I will do no such thing. The Hidden Realm will remain just that – hidden.'

'Please,' said Ling-Fei. 'The Hidden Realm is the last safe place for dragons to go. We want to help the dragons!'

Billy realized they hadn't yet explained to Glorious Old, or Glory, as she now wanted to be called, what was happening. 'You have to listen to us,' he said.

And, with a few interjections from his friends, he quickly told her what had happened.

By the end, Glory was staring at him sceptically. 'Is this really true?' she said. 'Our realm is falling into the Human Realm?'

'It is,' said Tank.

'It is a terrible thing for dragons to have to live amongst humans,' said Glory. She glowered at them. 'Even if you six human children seem to have good hearts, that does not mean all humans do. No, most humans have horrible hearts.'

'The Hidden Realm is the only option left for dragons,' said Billy. 'Please, you have to help us.' He could practically feel the opportunity to save the world slipping out of his fingers, and he clenched his fist as if that would stop it. 'Please.' His voice cracked.

Glory sniffed dismissively. 'And what do I care for the dragons of today? Not a single one of them tried to help me over thousands of years. No. I say let the humans and dragons destroy what is left of both of their realms. And when they are done, I will still be here, and I will have it all to myself. Both realms will belong only to me, and it will be so quiet and peaceful.' She closed her eyes, and as she did, her cloud form began to disappear.

'No!' Billy cried out, leaping up into the air and trying to grasp any part of her. He had to make Glory stay, had to make her understand, but his hands closed on nothing and he fell back to the ground.

Glory's eye opened again and she stared down at him quizzically. 'That was both spectacularly foolish and also quite brave.' She seemed intrigued, and Billy felt a flicker of hope that maybe, just maybe, they could convince her to help them.

'That's Billy in a nutshell,' muttered Dylan.

'Just give us a chance. You have to help us!' said Billy.

Sand began to whirl around them, until it rose up and took Glory's dragon shape. 'I do not have to do anything. I am the oldest dragon of all time. I may not have the ability to take a physical form, except for when I borrow from cloud, earth, fire or water, but I have powers beyond your understanding. If you knew what I do – the secrets of the universe – your small human brains would burst.'

'We don't want that,' Lola quickly interjected. 'We just want your help.'

Billy wracked his brain for how they could convince Glory to help them. *Spark*, he thought down their bond. *What do we do?*

I do not know, Spark thought back. *I did not expect her to be like this.*

'Great Glorious Old,' Spark said aloud. 'We have come so far to find you. To summon you. Surely that must show you that we are worthy of your help.'

At the word 'worthy', Glory lifted her great sand head, and her eyes lit up. 'Worthy,' she repeated. 'I have not met a worthy human ever. And even the dragons disappoint me now.'

Tank growled quietly in his throat.

Billy realized with a sudden certain clarity that they were going to have to change their approach.

'I don't believe you,' he said. 'You claim to be all-powerful, but if you're as powerful as you say you are, how come you're trapped here in this realm? How come you're not a star? I bet you weren't even that powerful when you were a dragon.'

He heard the sharp intake of breath from everyone

around him, but Billy was desperate. He needed this plan to work.

'Billy,' hissed Xing. He ignored her and ploughed on, staring straight at Glory.

'You're nothing now,' he said. 'You say that you're looking forward to the peace and quiet when humans and dragons have destroyed each other, but won't you be bored? Stuck here all on your own? We've come and offered you a chance to actually do something. If you really are so powerful and so all-knowing, then you'll know this is it. If we can't figure out a way for the realms to live in harmony, this is the end. Of everything.'

Billy's heart was hammering in his chest. He'd started the speech initially to goad Glory into helping them, but by the time he'd finished, he was speaking the truth. This would be the end if she didn't come on board. He wiped his sweaty palms on his super-suit.

The earth beneath them began to shake and Glory let out a loud cackling laugh. 'Oh, you foolish, foolish boy. Just because I have no physical control over my own body, and am merely a spirit, does not mean that I cannot control my surroundings.'

She shot up into the air, sand falling all around her, and then dived back down, this time in her cloud form. She whooshed straight at Billy and he flinched, waiting for an impact that never came. Instead, she went right through him, and as she did, he heard her voice whisper, 'I'll show you power.'

Spark shot out a lightning bolt to try to distract Glory, but with another laugh, she opened her cloud mouth and swallowed it. As she did, the bolt of lightning shifted and changed, taking on Glory's form.

'I can bend anything to my will,' she said, crackling with electricity.

Tank blew a burst of fire, and with another laugh, Glory took on a flame form. She was all fire, burning so brightly that Billy had to shield his eyes.

'You think I do not have power? I think whatever small taste of power you have had has made you bold. We shall play a game now, and you will see what true power looks like.'

Billy bit back his smile. If they were playing a game, there would be a winner. And if there was a winner, there could be a prize.

The wind around them began to pick up, sending sand flying into all their faces. The dragons made a circle round the children, trying to protect them, but the wind was too strong.

'What are the stakes of this game?' Billy cried out. 'We don't play for glory –' he paused, letting the word sink in – 'like you might be. We require a promise of true help.'

Glory shed her fiery form as easily as Billy might have taken off a jacket, and then she was nothing but glowing light, staring down at him.

'Very well. If you can beat me, in any game I choose, I will help you. But if you lose, you will stay here with me in the Dark Desert for ever.' She gazed at the rest of the group. 'All of you.'

Midnight let out a squeak.

'Oh, mate, maybe we should talk about this,' said Jordan anxiously.

But Billy was already nodding. 'It's a deal.'

Glory's Game

As Billy spoke the words, Glory smiled slowly, showing all of her glowing teeth. 'So it is done.'

'Billy! What were you thinking?' said Buttons. 'You should know better than to bargain with dragons.'

'He clearly was not thinking at all,' said Xing. 'But it is fine – it is not binding!'

'The boy spoke and so it is,' said Glory.

Billy swallowed, anxiety flooding him. He hoped he'd done the right thing. 'There's one of her, and twelve of us! Of course we can win any game.' He desperately hoped that was the case.

'Oh, you silly boy,' said Glory, her smile widening. 'Your dragons are not going to play.'

She slammed her tail, which was still made of light, against the sand of the Dark Desert below. Billy didn't expect anything to happen – after all, she'd said she had no real physical form – but as her tail hit the sand, a burst of energy exploded out of the earth, sending all twelve of them, humans and dragons, flying backwards.

Stars burst behind Billy's eyes as the impact of the energy blast ricocheted through his body. He was suddenly very afraid. He had been too cocky. Too bold. Now he was going to pay for it. And not just him, but his friends.

As the stars in his vision faded, he gasped. Billy and his friends were in the centre of a giant glowing circle, and outside it were their dragons. Billy knew that their dragons couldn't get in, and that they couldn't get out.

Not until the game was played.

It felt strangely familiar, and then Billy realized why. It reminded him of the tournament games that the Dragon of Death had made humans play in Dragon City.

'Dragons and their games,' he muttered to himself.

But this time, they were playing with so much more to lose.

Their dragons were frantic to get to them, but the glowing circle kept them out. Tank charged at the circle with a mighty roar, but he bounced straight off it, as if he were a tiny pebble being thrown against a glass window.

Xing hissed and dived, but whatever enchantment Glory had used stuck.

Spark, what's happening? Billy thought desperately. *You can get us out of here, right?*

You were too rash, Spark thought back. Billy heard the reproach in her tone, even though it was in his head. *I cannot save you now. You must play her game to save yourselves.*

Billy gazed around the Dark Desert. It was still pitch-black except for their glowing bodies and the ring of light where they were trapped. And above them, Glory soared. She burst in through the ring of light with another cackle. She was mostly made of air now – only the faintest shimmer of an outline showed her dragon form, though her eyes still glowed brightly.

'The benefit of being a spirit is, of course, that

nothing can keep me out,' Glory cawed, before flying back out again and circling the dragons gleefully. Billy watched as Neptune tried to snap at her with her enormous jaws, but they closed on empty air.

'Now, I may not be able to physically touch anything,' said Glory with another wide grin, 'but here, in the Dark Desert, where I drew my last breaths, I can bend the elements to my will.'

'I wish we'd known that before we made an unbreakable bargain with a dead dragon who's clearly both bitter and bored – a terrible combination,' said Dylan.

'Well, it's too little too late,' said Charlotte, crouching low on her heels, as if she were getting ready to propel herself upwards. 'We're here now, and there's no way I'm going to let a dead dragon defeat me.' She raised her chin defiantly. 'Come on, Glory. Show us what you've got.'

Lola laughed out loud, the joyful sound giving Billy an unexpected boost of confidence. 'Charlotte's right. Glory doesn't know what she's up against,' Lola murmured. 'We've got powers, and she's got some sand she can throw around.'

'Why must everything always end in battle,' said Ling-Fei with a sigh. 'Dear Glory, we'd prefer not to fight, but . . .' Her voice trailed off.

'But, if a battle is what you're after, a battle is what you'll get,' said Jordan.

'Yeah! Take that, you big old dead dragon!' said Dylan.

Glory snarled and Billy gulped. 'Too far, Dylan,' he whispered.

'Sorry,' said Dylan. 'I got caught up in the moment.'

'We don't want to battle you, but we do want to play the game that we were promised,' Billy called out.

The six friends moved together almost as one, forming a circle with their backs to one another. It filled Billy with strength.

Together you are strong, Spark's voice echoed in his head. *Stay together.*

'I do not remember small humans being so bold,' said Glory, eyeing them carefully.

'Well, you've been dead a long time,' said Lola. 'Things have changed.'

'Apparently,' said Glory. 'And my body may be dead,

but my spirit lives on, as does my power. Now I think I would like to show you just how powerful I am.'

She dived down and started circling them, moving faster and faster with every loop. Suddenly, trees exploded up out of the sand. Giant, leafy trees, all glowing in bright vibrant colours, the same way the neon crane had glowed.

At first, Billy was too amazed by the sight to realize what was happening, but then he saw that the trees were bursting up between him and his friends, trying to separate them.

'Stay together!' he shouted. He knew no matter what happened, they couldn't let Glory split them up. 'What kind of game is this anyway?' he yelled at the dragon spirit, who had now taken on the form of the leaves. Her enormous eyes stared out at Billy from underneath the foliage.

'It is simple. To win and show me you are worthy of being taken to the Hidden Realm, you simply have to catch me.' And with a burst of speed, she shot off through the magical forest. The trees parted to let her through until she reached the far end of the arena she'd created. Then she looked over her shoulder and laughed. 'Oh, and stay alive, of course.' The trees that had parted instantly snapped back into place, shrouding Billy and his friends in darkness.

There was a loud grumble from behind them, and Billy quickly looked over to see what was happening, before gasping. Shadow figures were rising up from the sand, figures with long claws and sharp teeth. They were stretching larger and larger, and snapping and reaching towards the children.

The friends drew closer together, and Billy felt a jolt run through him. He knew it was the power that came from them being together, the power that they'd always had since four of them had first opened Dragon Mountain together.

'You know what, I'd rather face those weird shadow creatures than the fanged rat creatures,' said Dylan.

'I don't think we need to face them at all. I think we need to stay away from them,' said Billy.

'I agree. They're distractions from our goal – catching Glory,' said Ling-Fei.

'Those aren't the only distractions,' said Jordan. 'Watch out!'

Huge boulders were now flying towards them, and

once again the trees swayed back and forth to let the rocks through.

'Where are they coming from?' said Lola in a panic.

'Never mind where they're coming from – we need to watch where they're going to land!' yelled Charlotte.

Ling-Fei brought her hands together and spun in a tight circle before planting her feet and thrusting her arms out towards the boulders, releasing a gale of wind. 'That should slow the boulders down!'

Charlotte sprang forward out of the group, and with ease caught two of the boulders. She lobbed them over her shoulder, walking back towards the shadow creatures. As each one landed on a shadow creature, both the creature and the boulder disappeared in a puff of smoke.

'That's weird,' said Dylan uneasily. 'Charlotte, did the boulders feel solid to you when you caught them?'

'Yep,' said Charlotte, staring at her hands. 'And, look, they even left dirt on my hands.'

'Glory has control over everything in here,' said Ling-Fei, her eyes darting around the glowing arena.

'There's so much magic and power, I can practically taste it.'

'We have to treat everything in here as though it's real,' said Billy. 'Glory can't touch us, or anything, for that matter, but she's able to create things that can.'

'Oh, children,' Glory called out from the edge of the arena, behind the glowing forest of neon leaves. 'Whatever are you waiting for? I told you – all you have to do is catch me.' She flashed them a wide grin. 'Perhaps I have made it too easy for you.' She whacked her tail on the ground again and then the earth began to rumble once more.

'Stay together!' Billy cried out, reaching for his friends' hands, but it was too late. Six pillars shot up out of the ground, thrusting the children into the air and away from each other.

Pillars Of Peril

The pillars spun skywards, up and up and up. 'Don't fall!' Billy cried out to his friends as he focused on maintaining his own balance.

'Easy for you to say!' Dylan yelled back. 'You have super agility!' But they all managed to stay on, even Dylan.

When they finally stilled, Billy and the others were so far up that the trees below them looked like pinpricks in the sand. He could also make out Glory perched on the far end of the arena, a thick, enchanted jungle stretching out between them. From what Billy could tell, Glory was miles away and they'd have to fight every step to get to her. Each pillar was only wide enough for one person to stand on, but Billy was relieved that they were at least close enough to reach out to each other.

He tried not to think about whether he'd made a huge mistake by pulling all of his friends into this mess. Shaking the thought from his mind, he clenched his fists. They were going to catch Glory. And they were going to get out of here, together.

'You know, if we ignore the circumstances, it's actually kind of peaceful up here,' said Ling-Fei, looking at the horizon. 'I mean, a neon jungle is a pretty spectacular sight.'

Lola rolled her eyes but she was smiling. 'You're always looking for the bright side, aren't you? But that's what ... I ... love ... about—' The pillars shook violently beneath them, cutting off Lola.

Down below, the shadow figures were leaping from the tops of the canopy onto the pillars. They were climbing and clawing up the wood so fast that chunks of the wood were being torn out as they ascended.

'Argh,' cried Charlotte. 'Why won't these darned shadow creatures just leave us alone?'

Dylan looked down, his hands trembling. Billy

saw him swallow hard before looking back up. 'Well, I think this is it. We've had a good run, friends. It was nice knowing all of you. Will it be death by shadow creature, or will we plummet into the neon jungle? My bet is that we fall. There's no way those shadow figures won't tear these pillars apart before they get to us.'

'Pull yourself together, Dylan! We've got out of worse before.' Lola leaned over and grabbed Jordan's shoulders. 'Use your power to get us down from here! I know it's new, so you don't know how to fully control it, but it's our only hope.'

Jordan's shoulders slumped and he shook his head. 'I . . . I . . . don't think I can do it. I've got to be able to see where I'm going, otherwise we might teleport *into* something, which I'm pretty sure would be a bad thing.'

'I don't know if we've got any other options,' said Charlotte, eyeing the shadow creatures, who were now halfway up the pillars.

Lola shook her head in frustration. 'I'm trying to slow them down with my power, but it doesn't seem to be affecting them for some reason.'

'I could try to use my wind powers to lower us down,' offered Ling-Fei, her voice small. 'But without a parachute or something to keep us in the air, I don't think we'd make it.'

Billy's heart sank further into his stomach. He couldn't accept this fate. Even if they didn't stand much of a chance, they still had to try.

Then an idea struck him.

'Ling-Fei, do you trust me?' he asked, offering her his hand.

She nodded.

'Get on my back. The rest of you, do everything you can to try to slow down those shadow figures.'

Ling-Fei leaped from her pillar onto Billy's back, wrapping her arms round Billy's neck.

'Hold on tight,' said Billy. 'We're going to have to move fast.'

And then he stepped off the pillar.

Billy quickly wrapped his arms round the pillar so he wouldn't fall to the ground, and they slid down it. He kept his legs straight and held his breath as they collided with the shadow figures, his feet easily knocking them off one side of the pillar and into the jungle below.

'It's working!' cried Billy as the shadow figures fell all around them. 'We're knocking them off!'

Billy was surprised that he could actually kick the shadow figures instead of passing straight through them, but he was relieved that his plan was working. He dug his hands into the pillar to slow them down as they approached the top of the canopy. There didn't seem to be any more figures here so Billy knew they had a safe place to stop. He quickly snagged a massive leaf from a nearby tree, which was big enough to be a hammock, and held each end of the leaf in the air above him.

'Okay, Ling-Fei. Here's your parachute. Let's fly.'

Ling-Fei was smiling as she filled their makeshift parachute with wind and lifted back into the sky. She kept one hand round Billy's neck, and the other outstretched to tame the wind.

'Took you guys long enough,' said Charlotte with a wink as Billy and Ling-Fei landed back on Billy's pillar.

'That was amazing, Ling-Fei!' said Dylan with a grin.

'Thanks,' Ling-Fei said. 'I have a feeling you used your charm on them too. How else did they all fall off?'

Dylan blushed. 'It was Lola's idea. She thought I should try to charm them into thinking the pillars were covered in ice and were too slippery to grip. Luckily it worked, but I don't know how much longer they're going to be fooled for.'

'I think we can all manage to fly away on this parachute,' said Billy. 'But I don't know if I'm strong enough to hold on for all of us.'

'Strength, you said? I've got us covered,' said Charlotte as she took the huge neon green leaf in her hands. 'Everyone, hop on.'

They took off towards the edge of the arena, Ling-Fei on Charlotte's back, Billy and Dylan holding onto Charlotte's legs and Lola and Jordan hooked round each of her arms. Together they flew across the arena.

'That was *amazing*,' said Lola.

'I can't believe we got away,' said Jordan.

'I know, and we're zooming over the trees! Of course the best way to get out of a magical neon jungle is to go over it, not *through it*. It's a no-brainer. We're going to reach Glory in no time!' said Dylan.

'I feel as if we can do anything,' added Ling-Fei,

her voice slightly strained from focusing on keeping their makeshift parachute on track as it floated through the air.

'Yes, it feels as if our powers are getting stronger,' said Billy.

Charlotte nodded in agreement. 'I think it's because we make each other stronger.'

The group were silent for a moment. Billy couldn't help but feel a bit ridiculous, floating through the sky with a leaf and his five best friends, but that was what he loved so much about their friendship – that they could be ridiculous, and that they could make up their own rules. He felt his powers surge within him – a tingling feeling that pulsed through his body.

'This is going to sound cheesy, but I really do feel as if we can do anything together,' said Billy.

'Oh, you bunch really are the sentimental type,' boomed Glory's voice from all around them. She was somehow projecting her voice everywhere in the arena. 'It is not a trait I care for, but I will admit I am surprised by your trust and teamwork. It appears I may have underestimated you children.' Billy could see Glory shaking her cloud head from afar. 'But I am not one to make mistakes twice. We shall see whether you are truly worthy.'

A flash of lightning suddenly split the sky open and rain poured from above, hammering down on their makeshift parachute. Then the wind around them became wilder, bucking them from side to side.

Billy could see the strain in Ling-Fei's face. 'Can you keep us in the air?'

'I think I can manage,' she said through gritted teeth. 'Our powers are stronger than they've ever been before, but it's going to take all of my energy to keep us going.'

'Good luck, human children,' said Glory.

With another crash of lightning, dozens and dozens of giant cranes appeared all around them. They weren't unlike the one the group had seen in the Cave of Secrets, but they were bigger, with sharper beaks and longer claws.

One dived straight at them from above, its claws stretched out in front of it.

'Those sons of biscuit-eaters are going to tear up our parachute!' cried Charlotte, who was still holding onto the leaf with both hands.

'We're defenceless!' cried Lola.

'Let me try something,' said Dylan, wrinkling his nose. A clone of Glory appeared in front of them. It let out a roar and a burst of fire. 'Be gone, little cranes! Be gone!'

Billy was impressed. Dylan had somehow been able to make all of the cranes think they were seeing Glory flying next to them.

The diving crane stopped momentarily, fluttering its wings in mid-air. Then it tucked its head downward again and dived towards them once more, shooting right through the image of Glory that Dylan had created.

'Well, I think I've somehow made it worse,' said Dylan.

'Don't worry,' said Jordan, his eyes bright. 'I've got an idea.' He reached his arm out to Lola. 'Grab my hand and do your time magic.'

Lola nodded and took his hand.

'We need some speed,' said Jordan, flashing a smile. 'Let's jump.'

They rocketed towards the ground like a shooting star, Lola's power propelling them faster than everything else. But before they struck the tree line, they disappeared with a loud *bang* and reappeared with another *bang* right above the diving crane. They crashed through the bird and it burst like an exploding ball of light.

Bang. Bang. Bang. Bang. Bang.

Jordan and Lola darted all around the sky, so fast it seemed as if they were everywhere at once. It was over in a matter of seconds. Before Billy could even process what had happened, all of the cranes exploded and the sky was full of fireworks.

Bang.

And then Jordan and Lola were back, holding onto Charlotte once more.

Jordan flashed his wide smile, braces glinting in the flickering light. 'You guys were right – our powers are stronger when we're together.'

Cheering, Billy and his friends flew to the edge of the arena, where Glory was waiting.

The Hidden Realm

As soon as the group reached Glory, the glowing arena disappeared. Spark, Buttons, Tank, Xing, Midnight and Neptune raced over to where the children were now standing.

'We won!' cried Billy. 'Now you have to show us where the Hidden Realm is.'

Glory grinned at him. 'Fine, I am impressed. I will show you the Hidden Realm, but only if you can keep up with me.' With a burst of speed, she shot out of the Dark Desert, leaving only wisps of clouds behind.

'That wasn't the deal!' Charlotte shouted after Glory as she vaulted herself up into the air and onto Tank's head.

'Can she break her word?' said Ling-Fei.

'Technically, she has not broken her word,' said Neptune. 'The game continues until you catch her.'

'That feels like cheating to me!' cried Midnight.

'Me too,' said Jordan as he hopped astride his dragon.

'You were great,' said Midnight proudly. 'I was cheering for all of you! How did you even manage to pull that off?'

'We'll tell you later,' said Billy, leaping onto Spark's back. 'Right now we have to follow Glory!'

'How can she be so fast?' said Dylan, clambering onto Buttons. 'She's only a spirit!'

'That is exactly why she is so fast,' said Xing as the group lifted up into the air and broke out of the black cloud that kept the Dark Desert dark, bursting into the true sky. 'It will be very difficult for us to catch her.'

'Look, there she is!' yelled Billy. 'Heading towards the horizon.'

They followed Glory across the sea, and on and on they flew, until Billy began to feel his eyes droop. But Glory was still just ahead of them, a little out of reach.

Then a strange thing began to happen. The horizon,

where the sky met the sea, began to grow closer. As it did, Glory finally started to slow down.

'Well done,' she said as they caught up with her. 'I did not think you would be able to catch me, but it appears dragons who have heart bonds are faster than most. Almost as fast as a spirit dragon.' She winked at them.

'But where's the Hidden Realm?' said Billy, looking around. 'This is still the Dragon Realm.'

'It is indeed,' said Glory. 'There is just one way into the Hidden Realm, but you can only go one by one.'

'Oh, it's going to take ages getting all the dragons in there,' said Dylan with a groan. 'So much for this world-saving plan.'

'Come on, think positively,' said Charlotte. 'Once we know where the Hidden Realm is, and how to get into it, I'm sure we can figure out a way to get more dragons in at once.'

Glory raised a cloud eyebrow. 'So confident.'

'Such is the way of humans, especially young ones,' said Xing.

'Glorious Old,' said Spark. 'We have summoned you, the children defeated you at your own game and we have flown as fast as you. Now it is time for you to hold up your side of the bargain.'

Glory looked at them. 'I cannot tell you what you will find in the Hidden Realm. It is not a place I go often. I do not like it, for it is cold.' Billy swallowed, suddenly nervous. What did Glory mean by 'cold'? Glory assessed all of them. 'Who will go first?'

'I will,' said Billy, trying to hide the tremor in his voice. He didn't want to leave his friends, but they were so close now to finding a haven for the dragons and saving everyone. And he wasn't going to let any of his friends risk their own safety. It had to be him – he was the one who'd bargained with Glory after all.

'I will follow,' said Spark. As she spoke, Billy felt braver. With Spark, he could face anything. He was sure of it.

'Then fly with me,' said Glory. 'But only you two. The rest will have their turn.'

'Shouldn't we stay together?' asked Ling-Fei. 'We always stay together.'

'I do not make the rules,' said Glory. 'Only one spirit must enter at a time.'

Something about that phrasing sent alarm bells ringing in Billy's head, but he silenced them. He had to see where and what the Hidden Realm was, so he could help lead the dragons safely there.

'I'll go,' Billy said again. 'And I'll be right back.' He turned to his friends. 'You guys stay together here. I'll see you soon.'

'I will stay with Billy,' said Spark. 'I will let no harm come to him.'

'Do not make promises you cannot keep,' said Glory. 'No creature can protect another from harm, as much as they may want to.'

'Well, I promise I will do my best,' said Spark.

'That's good enough for me,' said Billy, sending a burst of appreciation down their bond. He looked up at Glory. 'I'm ready.'

She assessed him again. 'You are very brave.'

'He is,' said Spark.

'Well, brave young human, fly with me,' said Glory. 'On your dragon, of course, as I cannot carry you.'

Glory, Spark and Billy flew on until the others became small specks in the distance, and then nothing at all.

'Are we there yet?' said Billy, trying to calm his beating heart.

'Fly as fast as you can towards the horizon line,' said Glory. 'There you will find the entrance to the Hidden Realm. It lies on the line between the horizon and the sky. I will go in first.'

Billy watched as Glory, still in her cloud form, raced ahead and slipped in between the sky and the sea, as if it were as easy as pulling open a curtain.

Spark flew Billy as close as she could, and he reached out and pulled on the edge of the sky. It came away with little resistance, and he saw there was a gap behind it.

The Hidden Realm.

Summoning all of his courage, Billy peeled back more of the sky and slipped off Spark's back and into the Hidden Realm.

At first, he was falling, and then he landed on ground that had a slight bounce to it, almost as though he'd dropped onto a giant trampoline, except he felt more weightless, as if he'd be able to float away at any given moment. The ground was covered by a swirling blanket of fog that licked at his knees. The fog seemed to have a mind of its own, circling around him to see if it could work him out.

As Billy studied the fog, something else dawned on him. It was completely and utterly silent. The Hidden Realm was the quietest place he'd ever been and it made him feel relaxed.

Billy swatted the air around him, momentarily clearing the fog, and gasped. There was no colour in the Hidden Realm – everything was black and white. But that wasn't what had caused him to catch his breath. Hovering all around him were hundreds and hundreds of *creatures*. Unearthly creatures that looked as if they'd been spawned in a nightmare and prised themselves out into the real world.

There was a snapping mouth the size of a car, skittering through the air on six legs. A monkey with eyes made of flame, wielding a long staff and floating on a cloud. A hand that was half-bone, half-flesh, feeling its way around as if it was searching for the rest of its body. And a bat with eight eyes, its cheeks hollow, exposing all of its fangs, even with its mouth closed.

Billy fought to push down the panic rising in

his chest and made himself as small and as still as possible, hoping nothing would notice him there. The creatures, if that was what things that seemed to only be half-alive could be called, looked like lost souls, the light behind their eyes empty as they snapped, clawed and slashed their way through the Hidden Realm, searching for something that Billy knew they'd never find.

Billy thought he might throw up. Their plan wasn't going to work. They'd never be able to convince dragons to live here in this decaying land of nightmares. He tried to tell himself that this might just be the entrance to the Hidden Realm. Surely the Hidden Realm held more than this, somewhere with light and colour and sound?

'Glory?' he whispered. 'Where are you?'

An eye opened up next to him. 'I am here, but I will not stay long. I do not like it here. It is far too cold.'

'It is cold,' Billy agreed, noticing that his teeth were starting to chatter. He looked down at his hands and frowned.

They were turning pale.

Not just pale, they were turning bone white.

He stared down at his super-suit, usually blue and black, and gasped. The colour was leeching out of it. 'What ... what's happening to me?'

Glory's eyes widened. 'I do not know. I have never brought a human in here. Or any living creature, for that matter.'

'And I feel ... funny,' said Billy. 'I feel sleepy and kind of empty.'

The light around Billy darkened, and he looked up to see a giant whale floating above them, its eyes bloated and its skin stretched tight as if it had been blown up like a balloon – so much so that it had floated out of a distant sea and into the Hidden Realm. Its body contorted as it opened its mouth, releasing a dark, swarming cloud of tiny insects. Then Billy heard the sound and he realized what he was seeing. They were locusts. Thousands and thousands of locusts. Their buzzing was a cacophony of sound in the previously silent realm.

'BILLY!' Spark was suddenly there. 'Billy, what is happening?' she cried over the ear-splitting buzz of the locusts. She whirled on Glory. 'Is this a trick? He is dying!'

'I'm what?' Billy mumbled sleepily.

'I can feel it through our bond!' Billy had never seen Spark so frantic. Her eyes were wild and lightning fizzed all around her, so violently that he thought she might explode.

Billy forced himself to speak, summoning all his energy to put his hand on his beloved dragon. 'Spark, something is happening to you too. Your colour, it's disappearing.'

'I fear you *both* may be dying,' said Glory. 'I did not know this place is only for the dead. I am already dead, of course.'

Billy opened his mouth to respond, but before he could speak, swarms of locusts rained down from above, shrouding him in darkness.

'Get back!' cried Spark, but her voice sounded far away. 'What are those things?'

'They appear to be some sort of life-sucking locust,' said Glory. 'They were sent by that strange whale.'

'Well, do something! Please!' Spark's voice broke. 'Glorious Old, I am begging you.'

'I cannot,' said Glory sadly. 'I have no power here, and now I know why. There is no life here, no magic – it is only suitable for the unliving. There is a reason why it is hidden from the living realms.'

Billy tried to pay attention to what Glory was saying, but all he could focus on was the locusts. They were everywhere, flying into his mouth, tangling themselves in his hair, crawling under his suit. They were nipping at his eyes and his ears, or maybe there were just so many of them swarming around him that he was actually only feeling the beating of their wings on his skin.

Billy swatted the air desperately as he fell to his knees, knocking huge swathes of locusts out of the way. But still they kept on coming, blocking out the light. He began to feel dizzy and faint, his vision growing dark around the edges. And then he felt himself begin to drift off to sleep, one that he knew he'd never wake from. Part of him knew he should be terrified, but as the locusts continued to swarm around him, all he wanted to do was to sleep. He had tried so hard, and come so far, but this was it. He thought about his parents, his friends and his dragon ... his dragon ... Spark! Spark was here! He used all of his remaining energy to send a burst of love down their bond.

As if from a long way away, he heard Glory's voice

as she spoke to Spark. 'The Hidden Realm is claiming him. It is too late to save him. Save yourself while you still can. The locusts will come for you next.'

'I will not let Billy die,' thundered Spark. She spoke so loudly that it jolted Billy awake for a moment. 'I am going to give him my life force, and then we are leaving here.'

Glory gasped. 'You would give him your life force? When you yourself are dying in here?'

But Spark wasn't listening, she was focused on Billy, and suddenly he felt a rush of warmth and love and life. As the life force burst around him, the swarming locusts started to disperse, and he blinked in the light. He finally felt as if he could breathe, as if he could *live*, and he lifted his head up.

'Spark!' he cried, his voice breaking as he realized how pale blue she was turning. 'Spark, you saved me!' He ran to her. He'd lost her once before to the Dragon of Death – he wasn't going to lose her again. Not ever.

'Glory, get us out of here, please!' he cried, as he held onto Spark's neck. 'It all looks the same to me!'

'You are quite the caring bunch,' she mused, before turning her back. 'This way.' She slipped through a crack Billy hadn't seen – a crack with light, glorious light, shining through it.

Billy got as close as he could, and then, using all of his strength, he wrenched the crack open. There, on the other side, was the sea and the sun and the sky of the Dragon Realm.

Spark's head drooped to the side. 'Come on, Spark, stay with me!' said Billy. 'We just need to figure out a way to get us out of here.'

Glory's eyes appeared in the crack. 'One by one, remember? I do not make the rules of this place.'

'Well then, Spark is going first,' said Billy, sliding off her back. Using all of his might, he pushed her through the crack, his strength buoyed by the burst of life force she'd sacrificed. Then, when she was all the way through, he dived after her, landing with a splash in the sea.

Freezing cold water went up his nose, but he didn't care, because the fact that he could feel it meant he was *alive*. He turned under the water and saw Spark next to him, in all her glorious colour. She swam beneath him, nudging him up towards the light, and they both burst up into the air, blinking in the sun.

Unlock Your Hearts

Billy clambered up on Spark's back and they flew up and out of the sea, sending droplets of water flying all around them.

'We have to tell the others!' Billy said, his voice hoarse. 'They have to know that the Hidden Realm isn't the solution! It isn't safe for dragons. It isn't safe for anyone or anything.'

He stared out across the sea, and in the distance, he could just about make out the shapes of the rest of the dragons and their human riders.

'I will summon them,' said Glory simply. Billy wasn't sure why she was suddenly being so helpful, but he was very glad of it. Glory closed her eyes, and several moments later, Buttons, Tank, Xing, Midnight and Neptune, along with the children, were next to Glory, Spark and Billy.

'How did we get here?' said Midnight.

'I am the oldest dragon in all existence. I can summon any dragon, at any time,' said Glory. 'My blood runs through all dragons. I may not be able to physically touch anyone or battle any longer, but when I call, they come.'

'Whoa,' said Lola. 'Cool power.'

'Indeed,' said Glory. 'And it is not the only power that I still have. But even my powers pale in comparison to the power of the heart bond.' She turned to Spark. 'I had forgotten the true power of the heart bond. Would you really have given your own spirit, your own life force, to save the human?'

'Billy saved me when I needed saving,' said Spark. 'I let him down once, and I will never do it again.'

'Hmm,' said Glory, watching them closely. 'You have made me realize how things could be.'

'I will not lie to you. Not every human has a good heart like these children do,' said Spark. 'Just as some dragons are not good. I have seen humans corrupted by greed who lash out at the world, but I have seen the hearts of many good humans too. There is more goodness than evil in the Human Realm.'

'Hmm,' said Glory again.

'It doesn't matter,' said Billy with a sigh. 'The Hidden Realm is unfit for dragons or humans.' He turned to his friends and explained what had happened there. How both he and Spark had nearly died, and that their heart bond was the only reason they were still alive. By the time he finished speaking, his voice shook with emotion. 'No matter what we do, there are dragons who refuse to live peacefully alongside humans, and humans who are intent on controlling or destroying dragons.' His eyes shone with tears. 'We failed.'

'Perhaps there is another way,' said Glory.

Billy frowned, confused. 'What do you mean? That was the last chance we had to bring peace between humans and dragons.'

'I believe I now know my destiny,' said Glory. 'Come, take me to the Human Realm. Let me see with my own eyes what is happening there.'

'What are you going to do when we get there?' said Dylan.

'As I told the girl,' said Glory, nodding at Lola, 'I have more powers than you know of. But enough talking. It is time to go back to your realm.'

'I will create a portal,' said Spark, bowing her head.

Billy felt a rush of hope flood through him, making his whole body tingle. There was something about Glory's words that made him feel as if maybe, just maybe, not everything was lost. Not yet. There was still a chance. There was still hope.

Billy looked around at the Dragon Realm, at the floating islands and the three moons and the oval sun. 'I guess this is goodbye to the Dragon Realm,' he said, his heart clenching as he realized he'd probably never see the Dragon Realm again. At least not like this, as a separate realm. Maybe the floating islands would fall into the Human Realm, or even one of the moons, but things would never be the same.

He knew now that nothing ever stayed the same – even his bond with his dragon and his friends. It was always changing and evolving.

'Are you ready?' said Spark.

'Yes, I'm ready. Let's go back,' replied Billy calmly.

And for what may have been the last time, Billy and his dragon leaped into a portal between realms.

The portal spat them out on the heath. As they tumbled out of it, Glory took on a new cloud form, and as the clouds formed her body, they turned lavender. The rest of the dragons and the children quickly emerged from the portal and landed next to Billy and Spark.

Billy looked around, trying to get his bearings, before realizing they were standing right above the Thunder Clan den. All around them, humans and dragons were battling.

'Oh no,' he whispered. 'Things are really bad. I hope we aren't too late.'

'Do not worry,' said Spark. 'Glory is on our side. She will help.'

'I hope so,' said Billy. It was one thing to talk about bringing peace to the world and another to put that plan into action, particularly now a huge battle was raging between humans and dragons in the Human Realm. Billy desperately hoped they could achieve what they'd set out to do.

To bring peace to both sides.

Thunder and Lightning must have sensed their return, because they suddenly flew out of the enchanted entrance of their den.

'Mum! Dad! I'm back!' cried Midnight, flying towards her parents.

'Midnight, darling!' said Lightning. 'We are so glad you are safe.'

'We are glad to see all of you are safe,' said Thunder in his rumbling voice. There was a loud oink of agreement and Goldie the pig flew out of Thunder's long, wispy beard.

'Goldie!' said Billy delighted. With another snort of joy, Goldie zoomed over to Billy and nuzzled his cheek.

'Did you find what you were looking for?' said Lightning. She looked up at Glory and gasped. 'And is this Glorious Old?'

Before they could respond, a new voice interrupted the reunion. A loud, angry voice.

'Get those dragons! We can definitely catch that little one!'

Billy looked over and saw a group of humans

wearing TURBO uniforms charging towards them. He immediately felt protective of Midnight, of all of the dragons. Even though he didn't want to add to the battle, he couldn't let TURBO attack them.

'Spark!' he cried. 'Can you handle that group of humans?'

'Of course,' said Spark, and she shot out an electric net that landed on them. The humans wearing TURBO uniforms shouted angrily, but they were trapped.

'We'll get you for this!' one yelled.

Goldie flew over and oinked in indignation at them before disappearing back into Thunder's beard.

'My, my,' said a voice close to Billy's ear. 'What a mess this all is!' Billy turned towards the voice and saw that Glory, still in her lavender cloud form, had flown close to him and Spark. She gazed around at the heath, at the battling dragons and the angry humans.

Then she turned her gaze to the city and the River Thames, and Billy knew she was seeing it all. Maybe she was even seeing further than London . . . seeing the entire world. She blinked and looked at Billy again.

'You are right – there is more goodness than evil,' she said. 'But both humans and dragons need to realize they can work together. I think I know how to do that.'

She flew high into the sky and began to grow in size. She grew and grew, her cloud form growing so big that it blocked out the sun itself.

When she spoke, her voice was heard by all. 'I am Glorious Old, and I am the first dragon. I was also the first dragon to be slain by a human.'

'Glorious Old has returned!' Billy turned at the familiar voice and saw a smug-looking Flame flying towards them, an entire clan of Dragons of Dawn flying behind it. 'Glorious Old will help us make a new world, only for dragons!'

'Do not speak for me,' said Glory, disdain dripping from her words. 'You did not summon me. You do not know why I am here.' She narrowed her eyes. 'And I do not care for dragons taking on the scale colour of each other. You forget that I can see inside each of your hearts, and many of them do not reflect your scales. I break the hold that your leader has on you.'

There was a sudden stillness and then lightning flashed in the sky. A moment later, the Dragons of

Dawn began to turn back to their original colours, before dispersing away from Flame.

'Flame,' said Tank. 'We believe you have kidnapped the human leaders. Release them, now.'

'I will do no such thing,' said Flame.

'You will, because you are right, this is a new world,' said Glory. 'A world where humans and dragons live in harmony. I was so angry at being betrayed by a human that I forgot about the power of the heart bond. I forgot that humans and dragons are stronger together.' She turned her gaze down on the humans and dragons assembled on the heath and beyond. 'I, Glorious Old, unlock your hearts. May you know the strength of the heart bond.'

Suddenly, streams of golden light poured out of humans and dragons alike. They shot into the air like fireflies, criss-crossing high in the sky.

'What's happening?' breathed Billy.

'Their hearts are calling out to their heart-bonded human or dragon,' said Spark. She nodded down at Billy's chest. 'Look.' Billy's heart was glowing, and he could see light connecting him and Spark. Him and his dragon.

'I will never bond with a human!' said Flame. 'Behold, my heart does not need a human!' But as it spoke, light began to shine out of it.

'It looks as if there is a human for you as well, Flame,' said Neptune with a smug grin.

Flame blinked at the light streaming out of its chest. 'But it cannot be.'

'You must open your heart,' said Glory. 'All of you. Humans and dragons alike. Open your hearts to the bond and to each other. Build a new and better world.'

Glory's cloud form began to shine, brighter and brighter. 'This was my destiny all along,' she called out. 'To return the world to the way it was before I was slain. Back to a time of peace between humans and dragons. Peace for all.' She shimmered so brightly, Billy had to shut his eyes, and when he opened them, she was gone.

Billy peered into the sky where a new star now shone, even though it was daytime. He knew, without a doubt, it was Glory. She'd finally achieved her destiny, and her spirit had been released to become a star, where she would watch over them for all of time.

A New World

After Glory had used her power to unlock all the heart bonds between humans and dragons, Flame had freed the prime minister, American president and Chinese president. The three world leaders were extremely displeased about having been kidnapped by dragons, but all in all they handled it with grace. Especially because they'd all had light shine out of them, so they knew that somewhere they had a heart-bonded dragon.

A summit was held where leaders from all over the world met with dragons. The world leaders signed a treaty stating that humans would not harm dragons. But the dragons who were representing their kind laughed and said they needed something more binding. 'Ink has no meaning to us,' they chuckled. 'It must be writ in flame and blood.'

And so, each world leader offered a drop of their blood, the dragons burned the paper that had been signed and everyone agreed that it was now unbreakable.

Of course, peace would not be as easy as signing a piece of paper (or burning one), but it was a good start.

The day after the summit, which was a week after Glory had unlocked the bonds, more and more dragons and humans were finding their heart-bonded partners. Now, Billy sat with his friends and their dragons on top of Parliament Hill, gazing down at London stretching out below them.

'So, what happens now?' said Dylan, laughing a little. 'We aren't special any more. Loads of people have heart bonds now.'

'And I heard some kids have been getting powers too,' said Jordan. 'Like me and Lola did.'

'How curious,' mused Buttons. 'I wonder ...' He trailed off.

'You wonder?' prompted Lola.

Buttons turned his gaze to Billy. 'Billy, when you were battling Frank Albert in the In-Between, the Forbidden Fountain was cut open, correct?'

Billy nodded. 'And then golden elixir spilled everywhere.'

'It is still there,' said Spark. 'Still flowing all throughout the In-Between. I saw it when we went through the soft spot.'

'Golden elixir is the pearls' source of power, which is, of course, what gave you all your powers in the first place,' said Buttons. 'And now there are holes between the realms, it's very possible that golden elixir is also spilling out, so children who have dragon heart bonds who come into contact with the elixir are gaining their own powers.'

Jordan laughed. 'But wouldn't I have noticed if I was suddenly doused in some sort of magic gold goop?'

'The golden elixir is extremely powerful and potent,' said Xing. 'Even small amounts in the air could awaken powers in someone who is heart-bonded to a dragon.'

'Wow,' said Lola. 'So we have our powers because we came into contact with golden elixir without even realizing it?'

'You have your powers because you have a heart bond with a dragon, and then the golden elixir awoke your powers so you can use them,' clarified Neptune. 'Without a heart bond, you may not have had a power. The heart bond comes first.'

'At least that's how we understand it,' said Buttons. 'Everything has changed now. I believe the world is going to be a very different place, for dragons and humans.'

'That's the understatement of the century,' said Dylan, grinning at his dragon.

'More kids with powers,' said Billy thoughtfully. What did that mean for the world? For the future? He imagined how confused those kids must be, suddenly having powers without any explanation. Not to mention being bonded with a dragon. 'We should try to find them,' he said, the idea coming on quickly. 'We can help them understand what's happening.'

'Yes, we're the original humans with heart bonds

and powers, after all,' said Charlotte with a wide smile. 'We know more about dragon bonds and powers than anyone.'

'I like the idea of helping others,' agreed Ling-Fei. 'We've always had each other, and I can't imagine going through any of this without all of you.'

'I like that idea too,' said Lola. 'We can show the newbies the ropes.'

'Didn't you just get your powers, like . . . yesterday?' said Dylan, grinning at her.

'I'm a quick learner,' said Lola with a smug smile.

'It's sorted then. We'll find the other kids and we'll help them,' said Billy. 'But we can do that tomorrow. Today, we celebrate.'

'Celebrate what?' said Dylan.

Billy gestured at the city below them. 'Celebrate all of this.' He lifted his head up to the sky where dragons flew peacefully. 'And this. We did that. We survived *and* we saved everyone.'

'We did it,' Charlotte repeated.

'We did it together,' clarified Ling-Fei with a huge grin.

'You will always be stronger together,' said Spark.

'Especially when we have our dragons with us,' said Lola, smiling at Neptune.

'We really have been through a lot,' said Dylan with a small laugh. 'This is definitely not what I thought I was signing up for when I arrived at a language and culture summer camp.'

Billy burst out laughing too. 'That's for sure,' he said, grinning at his friend. 'But I'm glad we were all in it together.'

'Imagine if we hadn't been in the same camp cabin!' said Dylan. 'Do you think any of this would have happened?'

'Oh, absolutely,' said Charlotte. 'We were meant to open Dragon Mountain.'

'I agree,' said Ling-Fei. 'We always would have found each other, and we always would have opened up the mountain and found our dragons.'

'You saved us,' said Spark quietly. 'More than once.'

'I mean, you all saved me too. Remember when Old Gold kidnapped me and literally trapped me in a tree?' said Dylan.

'Can we laugh about that now or is it still too soon?' said Charlotte, clearly holding back a giggle.

'Only if we can laugh about you being dragged underwater by a giant crab,' said Billy. 'That was back when I thought a giant crab was the scariest thing I'd ever seen.'

'That wasn't as bad as when I was nearly turned into stone!' said Charlotte with a shudder. But then she looked at Ling-Fei and Billy with a wide smile. 'And you two saved me. Remember how Ling-Fei literally held the earth open so Billy could find the Ember Flower?'

'I'm sure I helped too,' said Dylan.

'You did make us invisible when we sneaked into the Imperial Palace,' said Ling-Fei. 'That was incredibly useful.'

'See, I come in handy sometimes,' said Dylan.

'I still can't believe we found all eight pearls,' said Billy.

'And I cannot believe that I betrayed you all,' said Spark softly.

Billy put his hand on his dragon. 'It was all right in the end,' he said quietly. Because it had been.

'Are we at the part of the story where I come in now?' said Midnight, hopping up and down in excitement.

'Remember when I followed you and found out you were human children from another time?'

'And then you helped us defeat the Dragon of Death,' said Ling-Fei with a grin.

'I thought that would be the last time we had to save the world,' said Dylan. 'Shows how little I know!'

'Well, obviously you lot needed to find me and Lola,' said Jordan.

'We really did,' Billy agreed. 'And I'm so glad we met you both.'

'Billy, I'm still angry that you tried to convince me Neptune wasn't a dragon!' burst out Lola with a laugh. 'I knew what I'd seen!'

'I am glad you children found me,' said Neptune gruffly.

'Aw, Neptune!' said Lola.

'We are all glad to have been found,' said Tank.

'And without you children, perhaps we'd still be trapped in Dragon Mountain,' said Buttons.

'You saved us, and you saved everyone else,' said Xing. 'You are good children. Good humans. And you know I do not give praise unless it is deserved.'

'We've changed everything, haven't we?' said Charlotte.

'Indeed,' said Tank.

'Hopefully for the better,' added Ling-Fei.

As the enormity of what had happened this summer, the summer of Dragon Mountain, settled on them, they were all quiet for a few moments as they reflected.

'All we can do now is make this new world safe for all of us,' said Billy.

'Who knows what the future holds,' said Spark.

'Well, you are a seer dragon,' said Dylan. 'Maybe you could have a little peek?'

'No,' said Billy. 'Let's live in the moment. We can worry about tomorrow tomorrow.' He grinned at all his friends, and then at the dragons, and felt an overwhelming sense of peace and pride. 'I'm just glad that we're together.'

It was a new world, and Billy Chan and his friends and all their dragons were ready for whatever was to come.

ACKNOWLEDGEMENTS

We can't believe this is the fifth and final book (for now!) in the Dragon Realm series, and what an adventure it's been. It now feels as if writing *Dragon Destiny* was, indeed, always our actual destiny!

Our first thank you is to you, the reader, for coming along with us on the adventure. These books have changed our lives and we are so grateful. We've had so much fun dreaming up Billy, Spark and the gang, and to have been able to share them with readers around the world is truly a gift.

We're so lucky to have the most phenomenal team behind the books – our Dragon Dream Team! To our agent, Claire Wilson, who is fearless and kind and brave, and all of the qualities you want in a companion when you go on an epic quest. Thank you for everything. We also want to say hello to the dragon fans in her family, Tom and Oly.

Thank you to the rest of the team at RCW, especially Safae El-Ouahabi for all her support, and Sam Coates for taking our dragons global.

To the one and only Rachel Denwood, working with you is a privilege and a career highlight for us. Five books, can you believe it? We're so grateful that you decided to publish us and our dragons. Thank you for your vision and ambition for the series, and for making sure our dragons have soared. Long may we have reasons to go out for celebratory meals! And to Hector Haines, we hope you enjoy these books when you're older and are proud of your mum for making them a reality (along with so many other amazing books).

Thank you to the amazing Amina Youssef, who is the true hero of this book. We quite literally could not have finished *Dragon Destiny* without your excellent editorial insight and guidance. We love working with you. Thank you for your kindness and most of all thank you for helping us write a book that we're proud of. Cheers to more bookish adventures ahead!

We've now written many books, so we know without a doubt that the best copyeditor in the business is Catherine Coe, and we're so lucky to have her as *our* copyeditor! Thank you, Catherine, for helping us figure out our dragon battle logistics and for always understanding the jokes. Please always copyedit our books for ever and ever! We would also like to thank our eagle-eyed proofreader, Leena Lane.

While we are very proud of the words inside our books, what we love most about them are the incredible covers! A huge thank you to the absurdly talented Petur Antonsson for the cover illustrations. They're iconic! We cannot imagine our books without your artwork. Thank you as well to the design team at S&S, especially David McDougall and Jesse Green.

Our dragons are always soaring to new heights thanks to the wonderful sales, marketing and PR teams at Simon & Schuster. We're blown away by your creativity, enthusiasm and brilliance! We'd especially like to thank Laura Hough, Dani Wilson, Sarah Macmillan, Ian Lamb, Dan Fricker, Eve Wersocki Morris and Sarah Garmston.

The audiobooks are fantastic (we really recommend

them!) – thank you to Dominic Brendon at Simon & Schuster and our narrator, Kevin Shen, for making them so epic. Sorry that we're always adding new characters for you to voice!

We're incredibly grateful to booksellers for being so amazing and always supporting the series! We'd like to especially thank Queens Park Books, Muswell Hill Children's Bookshop, Pickled Pepper Books, Chicken and Frog Bookshop, Stories by the Sea, Tales on Moon Lane and Waterstones for their support.

We also want to thank all the amazing teachers and librarians who have introduced the books to their students. You are heroes!

We're very lucky to have so many wonderful friends to cheer on our dragons – thank you to Cat, Kiran, Tom, Anna, Kate, Abi, Katherine, Roshani, Krystal, Alwyn and Samantha.

We'd also like to thank our friends Jeni, Maarten, Kris and Dyna, as well as their wonderful small humans – Matilde, Lyra and Mylo.

To our wonderful family across the globe. A dragon-sized thank you to the Tsang, Webber, Hopper and Liu family members for their support and enthusiasm, and for always being excited for us. We especially want to thank Kevin's parents, Paulus and Louisa Tsang, and Katie's parents, Rob and Virginia Webber, for always supporting us. To Kevin's sister, Stephanie, her husband, Ben, and our nephew, Cooper, you guys are our favourite dragon fans! And to Katie's sister, Janie, her brother, Jack, and Jack's fiancée, Cat, thank you for brainstorming with us and cheering on every dragon adventure.

And, finally, to our darling daughters. To Evie, who we were pregnant with when we started writing the first book, and to Mira, who came into the world between *Dragon City* and *Dragon Rising*. You two are our biggest adventure and our greatest joy. We love you always.

KATIE & KEVIN TSANG met in 2008 while studying at the Chinese University of Hong Kong. Since then they have lived on three different continents and travelled to over 40 countries together. As well as the DRAGON REALM series, they are the co-writers of the young fiction series SAM WU IS NOT AFRAID (Egmont) and Katie also writes YA as Katherine Webber.

Have you read?

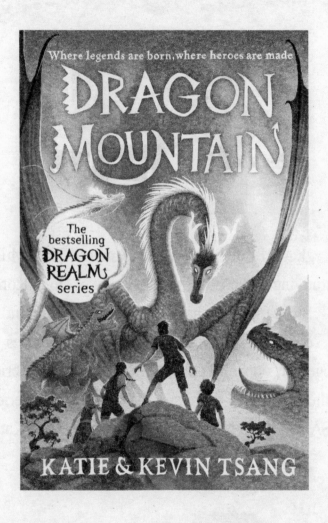

Have you read?

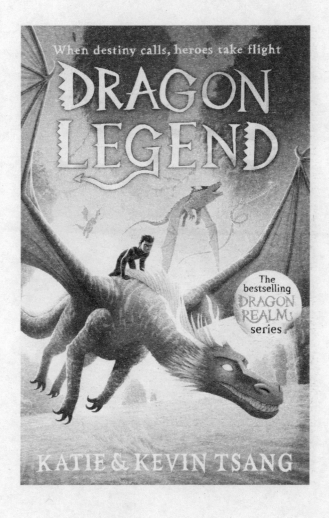

Have you read?

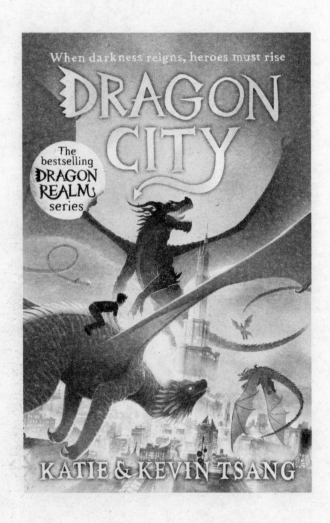

Have you read?